The Satanic Mill

The Satanic Mill

Otfried Preussler

TRANSLATED BY ANTHEA BELL

COLLIER BOOKS
Macmillan Publishing Company   New York

Collier Macmillan Canada   Toronto
Maxwell Macmillan International Publishing Group
New York   Oxford   Singapore   Sydney

Second Collier Books edition 1991
First Collier Books edition 1976

Copyright © 1971 by Otfried Preussler
Translation copyright © 1972 by Abelard-Schuman Ltd.

Collier Books
Macmillan Publishing Company
866 Third Avenue
New York, NY 10022

Collier Macmillan Canada, Inc.
1200 Eglinton Avenue East
Suite 200
Don Mills, Ontario M3C 3N1

First published in German by Arena-Verlag
First published in English by Abelard-Schuman Ltd., London

Printed in the United States of America

1 2 3 4 5 6 7 8 9 10

Library of Congress Cataloging-in-Publication Data
Preussler, Otfried.
    [Krabat. English]
    The Satanic mill / by Otfried Preussler; translated by Anthea
Bell. — 2nd Collier Books ed.
        p.   cm.
    Translation of: Krabat.
    Summary: In seventeenth-century Germany, a boy desperately wants
to escape from a school for Black Magic where he is held captive by
demonic forces.
    ISBN 0-02-044775-2
    [1. Witchcraft—Fiction.   2. Occultism—Fiction.]   I. Title.
PZ7.P9245Sat 1991 [Fic]—dc20   90-26306   CIP   AC

CONTENTS

THE
FIRST
YEAR

1 · THE MILL

IT WAS between New Year's Day and Twelfth Night, and Krabat, who was fourteen at the time, had joined forces with two other Wendish beggar boys. Although His Most Serene Highness the Elector of Saxony had passed a law forbidding vagabonds to beg in His Most Serene Highness's lands (but luckily the justices and those in authority would often turn a blind eye), the boys were going from village to village in the country around Hoyerswerda, dressed as the Three Kings from the East. They wore straw crowns on top of their caps, and one of them, little Lobosch from Maukendorf, who was playing the part of the King of the Moors, blackened his face with soot every morning. He walked proudly at the head of the little procession, bearing the Star of Bethlehem, which Krabat had nailed to a stick.

Whenever they came to a farm, they would put Lobosch in the middle and sing, "Hosanna to the Son of David!" Or rather, two of them would sing, while Krabat merely moved his lips silently, because his voice was breaking. The other two Kings sang all the louder to make up for it.

A good many farmers had killed a pig for the New Year, and they would give the Three Kings from the East plenty of sausages and bacon. At other houses they got apples, nuts and prunes, and sometimes gingerbread and lardy cake, aniseed balls and cinnamon cookies.

"Here's a good start to the year!" said Lobosch at the end of the third day. "I could go on this way till next New Year's Eve!"

Their Majesties the other two Kings nodded solemnly and sighed, "We wouldn't mind that at all!"

They spent the next night in the hayloft of the smithy at Petershain, and it was there that Krabat dreamed his strange dream for the first time.

There were eleven ravens sitting on a perch, looking at him. He saw an empty place down at the end of the perch, on the left, and then he heard a voice. It was a hoarse voice, and it seemed to be coming out of thin air, from very far away, and it called him by his name, but he did not dare reply. "Krabat!" called the voice a second time, and then a third time—"Krabat!" Then it said, "Come to the mill at Schwarzkollm, and you will not regret it!" At these words the ravens rose from their perch, croaking, "Obey the voice of the Master! Obey!"

With that, Krabat woke. "What a strange dream!" he thought, turning over and dropping off to sleep again. The next day he and his companions walked on, and when he happened to think of the ravens, he laughed.

However, he dreamed the same dream again the next night. Once more the voice called him by his name, and once more the ravens croaked, "Obey!" This set Krabat thinking, and the next morning he asked the farmer who had given them shelter for the night if he knew of a village called Schwarzkollm, or some such name.

The farmer remembered hearing that name. "Schwarzkollm . . ." he said reflectively. "Oh, yes—it's in the forest of Hoyerswerda, on the road to Leippe! There's a village called Schwarzkollm there."

The Three Kings spent the next night in a barn in Gross-Partwitz, and there too Krabat dreamed his dream of the ravens and the voice that seemed to be coming out of thin air. Everything happened just as before, and now he made up his mind to follow the voice. He crept out of the barn at daybreak, while his companions were still asleep. At the gate of the farmyard he met the servant girl going to the well. "Say good-by to my two friends for me," he asked her. "I have to leave them now."

At every village he came to, Krabat asked the way. The wind drove the falling snow into his face, and he kept having to stop and wipe his eyes. He got lost in the forest of Hoyerswerda, and it took him a good two hours to find the road to Leippe again. So it was that he did not reach his journey's end until nearly evening.

Schwarzkollm was like any of the other moorland villages, with a long line of houses and barns on either side of the street, which was deep in snow. Plumes of smoke rose above the rooftops, and Krabat saw steaming middens and heard the lowing of cattle. There were children skating on the duck pond, shouting with glee.

Krabat looked around for a mill, but he could not see one. There was an old man carrying a bundle of sticks coming up the road, and Krabat asked him.

"No, there's no mill in this village," he was told.

"Is there one nearby?"

"Oh, if *that*'s the one you mean . . ." The old man jerked a thumb over his shoulder. "Back there in the fen of Kosel, by the Black Water, there's a mill. But . . ." And he broke off as though he had already said too much.

Krabat thanked him and turned in the direction the old man had pointed. He had gone only a few paces when he felt someone pluck him by the sleeve, and when he looked around, it was the old man with the bundle of sticks again.

"What is it?" Krabat asked.

Coming closer and looking cautiously around, the old man said, "I just wanted to warn you, boy! Keep away from the Kosel fen, keep away from the mill by the Black Water—it's a queer place, that . . ."

Krabat hesitated for a moment; then he turned from the old man and went on his way, out of the village. Dusk was gathering, he had to take great care not to stray from the path, and he was shivering with cold. When he turned his head he saw lights begin to flicker in the village he had left behind, here one, there another.

Might it not be wiser to turn back?

"Oh, come!" muttered Krabat, pulling up his collar. "I'm not a baby! It won't hurt just to take a look at this mill!"

For some time Krabat groped his way blindly through the wood, until he came upon an open space. As he was emerging from the trees the clouds cleared away, the moon came through, and suddenly everything was flooded in cold moonlight.

Then he saw the mill.

It lay there before him, a hunched shape in the snow, dark and menacing, like some vicious, powerful animal lying in wait for its prey.

"I don't *have* to go there," thought Krabat, but then, telling himself he was a coward, he plucked up his courage and stepped forward out of the shadows of the wood. Striding boldly up to the mill, he found the door of the house closed, and knocked.

He knocked once, he knocked twice; there was no movement inside the house. No dog barked, no step creaked, no bundle of keys rattled—nothing.

Krabat knocked for the third time, so hard that it hurt his knuckles.

All was still quiet inside the mill. He tried the door handle, and the door opened. It was not even bolted. Krabat walked into the hall of the house.

It was silent as the grave, and pitch dark. But right at the end of the passage there was a faint gleam of light, just the glimmer of a glimmer.

"There's sure to be someone around, if there's a light," said Krabat to himself.

Arms outstretched, he groped his way forward. As he came closer he saw that the light was coming through a chink in the door at the end of the passage. Suddenly full of curiosity, he crept up to the chink on tiptoe and peered through it.

He saw a room lit by the light of a single candle. The room was all black, and the candle red; it was stuck in a skull that lay on a table in the middle of the room. Behind the table sat a burly man in dark clothes. His face was very pale, white as a sheet, and he had a black patch over his left eye. A thick, leather-bound book lay chained to the table in front of him, and he was reading this book.

Suddenly he raised his head and gazed across the room, as if he had detected Krabat behind the chink in the door. His glance froze the boy to the marrow of his bones. Krabat's eye, glued to the chink, began to itch, and then to stream, and his view of the room blurred.

Krabat rubbed his eye—then he felt a cold, icy hand placed on his shoulder from behind. The chill of it went right through his coat and his shirt. At the same time he heard a hoarse voice say, in the Wendish language, "So here you are!"

Krabat jumped; he knew that voice. When he turned around, he was facing the man with the patch over his eye.

How had he gotten there? One thing was certain, he had not come through the door . . .

The man, who was holding a candlestick in his hand, looked Krabat up and down in silence. Then, thrusting out his chin, he said, "I am the Master of this mill. You can be my apprentice if you like—I'm in need of one. Would you like that?"

Krabat heard himself reply, "Yes, I would." His voice sounded strange, as if it did not belong to him at all.

"And what am I to teach you? How to grind grain, or the rest as well?" inquired the master miller.

"The rest as well," said Krabat.

The miller held out his left hand.

"Done!"

At the very moment that they shook hands, a muffled thudding and rumbling sound started up somewhere in the house. It seemed to come from deep down. The floor quivered, the walls began to tremble, the beams and doorposts shook.

Krabat cried out and tried to run. All he wanted was to get away from this place! But the miller barred his way.

"The mill!" he cried, cupping his hands around his mouth. "The mill is grinding again!"

2 · ELEVEN AND ONE

SIGNALING to Krabat to follow him, the Master silently showed the boy the way up the steep wooden stairs to the attic where the miller's men slept. In the light of the candle Krabat could make out twelve low truckle beds with straw mattresses, six on one side of the room, six on the other, and beside each a locker and a pinewood stool. The blankets on the beds were tumbled, there were a couple of overturned stools in the gangway between them, and shirts and stockings were flung around the room. It looked as though the miller's men had been summoned posthaste to work, straight from their beds.

One bed, however, was untouched, and the Master pointed to a bundle of clothes at its foot. "There are your things," he said. Then he turned and went out, taking the candle with him.

Krabat was left alone in the dark. Slowly, he began to undress. As he took off his cap, he felt the straw crown—why, it was only yesterday he had been one of the Three Kings! How long ago that seemed!

The attic too was echoing with the thud and clatter of the machinery of the mill, and it was lucky for the boy that he was worn out. No sooner did he lie down on his straw mattress than he fell asleep, and he slept like a log.

He slept and slept, until suddenly he was awakened by a ray of light.

Krabat sat up, and froze with horror.

There were eleven white figures standing around his bed, looking down at him in the light of a stable lantern. Eleven white figures with white faces and white hands.

"Who are you?" asked the frightened boy.

"We are what you will soon be," one of the apparitions replied.

"We won't hurt you," another of them added. "We are the miller's men; we work here."

"There are eleven of you?"

"And you make twelve! What's your name?"

"Krabat. What's yours?"

"I am Tonda, the head journeyman. This is Michal, this is Merten, this is Juro . . ."

Tonda introduced them all by name, and then said, "That's enough for now. Go back to sleep, Krabat. You'll need all your strength in this mill."

The miller's men went to their truckle beds, the last one put out the light, they said good night and soon they were all snoring.

At breakfast the miller's men assembled in the servants' hall of the house, where the twelve of them sat around a long wooden table. There was good, thick oatmeal, one large dish to every four men. Krabat was so hungry that he fell on it ravenously. If dinner and supper were as good as breakfast, this mill was not a bad place at all!

Tonda, the head journeyman, was a handsome fellow with thick, iron-gray hair, though judging by his face he could hardly be thirty years old. There was something very grave about Tonda, or more precisely, about his eyes. Krabat trusted him from the first; his calm manner and the friendly way he treated the boy made Krabat take to him at once.

"I hope we didn't give you too bad a fright last night," said Tonda, turning to him.

"Not too bad!" said Krabat.

And when he saw the "ghosts" by daylight, they were just young men like any others. All eleven spoke Wendish, and they were some years older than Krabat. When they looked at him it seemed to him there was pity in their eyes, which surprised him, but he thought no more about it.

What did puzzle him was the way the clothes he found at the end of his bed, though secondhand, fitted as if they had been made for him. He asked the others where they got their things—who had worn them before? But the moment his question was out, the miller's men put down their spoons and gazed sadly at him.

"Have I said something wrong?" asked Krabat.

"No, no," said Tonda. "Your clothes . . . they belonged to the man who was here before you."

"Why did he leave?" asked Krabat. "Has he finished his apprenticeship?"

"Yes," said Tonda. "Yes . . . he has finished his apprenticeship."

At that moment the door flew open, and the Master came in. He was angry, and the miller's men shrank back from him.

"No idle chatter here!" he shouted at them. His one eye fell on Krabat, and he added harshly, "It's a mistake to ask too many questions. Repeat that!"

"It's a mistake to ask too many questions," Krabat stammered.

"Get that into your head, then!"

And the Master left the servants' hall, slamming the door behind him.

The men began to eat again, but suddenly Krabat felt he had had enough. He stared down at the table, bewildered. No one was taking any notice of him.

Or were they?

When he looked up, Tonda glanced across the table and nodded to him—very slightly, but the boy was glad of it. He could feel that it was good to have a friend in this mill.

After breakfast the miller's men went to work. Krabat left the servants' hall along with the others. The Master was standing in the hall of the house, and he beckoned to Krabat, saying, "Come with me!"

Krabat followed the miller out of doors. The sun was shining, it was a cold, still day, with hoarfrost on the trees.

The miller took him behind the mill, to a door at the back of the house, which he opened. They both entered the meal-store, a low-ceilinged place with two tiny windows covered with flour dust. Flour covered the floor too, hung on the walls, lay thick on the oak beams of the ceiling.

"Sweep it out!" said the Master, pointing to a broom beside the door. He went away, leaving the boy alone.

Krabat set to work, but after wielding his broom a few times he was enveloped in a thick cloud of flour, like dust.

"I'll never do it this way," he thought. "Once I get to the other end of the room it will be as thick as ever back here! I'd better open a window."

The windows were nailed up from outside, the door bolted. He might rattle it and bang on it as hard as he liked, it was no good. He was a prisoner here.

Krabat began to sweat. The flour stuck to his hair and eyelashes, it tickled his nose, it roughened his throat. It was like an endless nightmare—flour and more flour, great clouds of it, like mist, like flurrying snow.

Krabat was breathing with difficulty; he laid his forehead against a beam. He felt dizzy. Why not give up?

But what would the Master say if he just put down his broom now? Krabat did not want to get into the Master's bad books, not least because of the good food at this mill. So he forced himself to go on, sweeping from one end of the room to the other without stopping, hour after hour.

Until at last, after half an eternity, someone came and opened the door. It was Tonda.

"Come along!" he cried. "It's midday!"

The boy did not wait to be told twice. He staggered out into the fresh air, gasping for breath. The head journeyman glanced inside the meal store.

"Never mind, Krabat," he said, shrugging his shoulders. "No one does any better at the start!"

Muttering some words that Krabat did not catch, he traced something in the air with his hand. At that, the flour in the room rose up in the air, as if a strong wind were driving it out of every nook and cranny. A white, smoky plume swept out of the door and away over Krabat's head, toward the wood.

The room was swept clean; not a grain of dust was left behind. The boy's eyes widened in amazement.

"How did you do that?" he asked.

Tonda did not reply, but only said, "Let's go in, Krabat; the soup will be getting cold."

3 · NO BED OF ROSES

KRABAT had a hard time from then on. The Master worked him unmercifully. It was, "Where are you, Krabat? There's a couple of sacks of grain to be carried to the granary," and "Come here, Krabat! You're to turn the grain over, right from the bottom, so it won't start sprouting!" or "That meal you sifted yesterday is full of husks! You'll see to it after supper, and no bed for you before it's clear of them!"

The mill in the fen of Kosel ground grain every day, weekdays and Sundays, from early in the morning until night began to fall. Only once a week, on Fridays, did the Miller's men stop work earlier, and they started two hours later than usual on Saturdays.

When Krabat was not busy carrying sacks or sifting meal, he had to chop wood, shovel snow, carry water to the kitchen, groom the horses, cart manure out of the cowshed—in short, there was always plenty for him to do, and when he lay down on his straw mattress at night, he felt as if every bone in his body was broken. His back was aching, the skin of his shoulders was chafed, and his arms and legs hurt so much he could hardly bear it.

Krabat marveled at his companions. They did not seem at all bothered by the heavy day's work; none of them appeared tired or complained. They did not even sweat or get out of breath as they worked.

One morning Krabat was busy clearing snow from the way to the well. It had snowed all night without stopping, and the wind had drifted up the pathways. Krabat gritted his teeth; every time he dug his shovel in he felt a sharp pain in his back. Then Tonda came up to him, and looking around to make sure they were alone, he put a hand on Krabat's shoulder.

"Keep going, Krabat . . ."

Suddenly the boy felt as if new strength were flowing into him. The pain vanished, he seized his shovel, and would have gone on shoveling away with a will if Tonda had not taken his arm.

"Don't let the Master notice," he said. "Nor Lyshko either!"

Krabat had not liked Lyshko much from the first; he was a tall, lean fellow with a sharp nose and a squint, who seemed to be a snooper and an eavesdropper and a creeper around corners—you could never be sure you were safe from him.

"All right," said Krabat, and he went on with his work, acting as though he were making very heavy weather of it. Quite soon, as if by chance, along came Lyshko.

"Well, Krabat, how do you like the taste of your job?"

"How do you think?" grumbled the boy. "You try a nice mouthful of dirt, Lyshko—that's about how much I like the taste of it!"

After this, Tonda took to meeting Krabat more often and placing a hand unobtrusively on his shoulder. Every time, the boy felt new strength coursing through him, and however hard his work might be, he found he could do it easily.

The Master and Lyshko knew nothing at all about it—nor did the other miller's men, not the two cousins Michal and Merten, each as strong and good-natured as the other, nor pockmarked Andrush, who was a great joker, not Hanzo, who was nicknamed "The Bull" because of his bull neck and his close-cropped hair, nor Petar, who passed his spare time whittling wooden spoons, nor the popular Stashko, who moved quick as a flash and was as clever as the little monkey Krabat remembered gaping at years before, at the fair in Koenigswartha. Kito, who always looked as if he had just swallowed a pound of nails, noticed nothing either, nor did the silent Kubo—nor, of course, did stupid Juro.

Juro was a brawny young man with short legs and a flat moon face sprinkled with freckles. He had been there longer than anyone but Tonda. He was not much use at the work of the mill, being, as Andrush used to say mockingly, "too stupid to keep bran and flour apart," and but for the fact that he had fool's luck he would certainly have fallen into the machinery and been caught between the millstones long ago, said Andrush.

Juro was quite used to such remarks, and put up with Andrush's teasing patiently; he ducked without protest when Kito threatened to hit him for some trifle or other, and when, as often happened, the other journeymen played a practical joke on him, he took it with a grin, as much as to say, "Well, I know I'm stupid!"

The housework seemed to be all Juro was fit for, and since someone had to see to it, they were all perfectly happy to let Juro do it for them: cooking, and washing the dishes, baking bread and lighting fires, scrubbing the floor and scouring the steps, dusting, washing, ironing and everything else that had to be done about the house and the kitchen. He looked after the chickens, geese and pigs too.

It was a mystery to Krabat how Juro ever got all his jobs done. However, it seemed perfectly natural to the others, and on top of that, the Master treated Juro like dirt. Krabat thought it was a shame, and once, when he took a load of firewood into the kitchen and Juro, not for the first time, gave him the end of a sausage to put in his pocket, he told him exactly how he felt.

"I just don't see how you can put up with it!" he said.

"What, me?" asked Juro in surprise.

"Yes, you!" said Krabat. "The Master treats you shamefully, and all the others laugh at you!"

"Tonda doesn't," Juro objected. "You don't either."

"What difference does that make?" cried Krabat. "I know what I'd do if I were you. I'd stick up for myself, that's what! I wouldn't take it any more—I wouldn't take it from Kito or Andrush or any of them!"

"Hm," said Juro, scratching the back of his neck. "Maybe that's what *you*'d do, Krabat—well, you could! But what if you were just a fool like me?"

"Well, run away, then!" cried the boy. "Run away from here! Find somewhere else where they'll treat you better!"

"Run away?" And for a moment Juro did not look stupid at all, merely tired and sad. "Try it, Krabat! Try running away from here!"

"I don't have any reason to!"

"No," muttered Juro, "no, of course you don't—let's hope you never do . . ."

He put a crust of bread in the boy's other pocket, cut short his thanks and pushed him out of the door, a silly grin on his face just as usual.

Krabat saved his bread and sausage until the end of the day. Soon after supper, while the miller's men were sitting in the servants' hall, Petar busy with his whittling and the rest passing the time by telling stories, the boy left them and climbed up to the attic, where he threw himself down on his straw mattress, yawning. He ate his bread and sausage then, and as he lay there enjoying his feast, his thoughts went back to Juro and their talk in the kitchen.

"Run away?" he thought. "Run away from what? It's no bed of roses here, with so much hard work to do, and I'd be in a bad way without Tonda's help. But the food's good, there's plenty of it, I have a roof over my head—and when I get up in the morning I'm sure of a bed for the next night, warm and dry and reasonably soft, with no bugs or fleas in it. That's more than I could ever have hoped for when I was a beggar boy!"

4 · A DREAM
OF ESCAPE

KRABAT had run away once in his life already, soon after the death of his parents, who had died of the smallpox the year before. The pastor had taken him in, "to stop the child running wild," said he, which was much to the credit of the good pastor and his wife, who have always wished for a boy of their own. But Krabat, who had spent all his life in a wretched hovel, the shepherd's hut at Eutrich, found it hard to settle down in the pastor's house and be good all day long, never shout or fight, wear a white shirt, wash his neck and comb his hair, not go barefoot, keep his hands clean and his fingernails scrubbed —and on top of all that he had to speak German the whole time instead of Wendish!

Krabat had tried as hard as he could. He tried for a whole week, and then another week, and after that he ran away from the pastor's house and joined the beggar boys. He was not absolutely certain that he wanted to stay at the mill in the fen of Kosel for good, either.

"All the same," he decided, licking his lips as he finished the last morsel, and half asleep already, "all the same, when I run away from here it'll have to be summertime . . .

no one's getting me to leave before the wild flowers are out, and the wheat's springing in the fields, and the fish in the millpond are biting . . ." .

It is summer, the wild flowers are out in the meadows, the wheat is springing, the fish in the millpond are biting. Krabat has quarreled with his master; instead of carrying sacks of grain he lay down in the grass in the shadow of the mill and fell asleep, and the Master caught him at it and hit him with his big stick.

"I'll teach you to be idle in broad daylight, young man!" the miller shouted.

Was Krabat to put up with such treatment? In winter, with the icy wind howling over the moor, perhaps he'd have to take it. Aha—the Master was forgetting that it's summer now!

Krabat has made up his mind. He won't stay in this mill a day longer! He steals into the house, takes his coat and cap from the attic, and then slips away. No one sees him. The Master has gone back to his own room, the blinds are down over the windows because of the hot weather, the miller's men are at work in the granary and tending the millstones, even Lyshko is too busy to bother about Krabat. Yet the boy still feels that someone is secretly watching him.

When he looks around, he does see a watcher on the woodshed roof, sitting there staring at him—a rough-haired black tom cat, a cat that doesn't belong in the mill. It has only one eye.

Krabat bends to pick up a stone, throws it at the cat and shoos it off. Then he hurries toward the millpond, under cover of the willows. He catches sight of a fat carp in the water by the bank. It is goggling up at him with its one eye.

Feeling ill at ease, the boy picks up a stone and flings it at the carp, which dives away, plunging down into the green depths of the pond.

Now Krabat is following the Black Water to that place in the fen of Kosel that folks call the Waste Ground. He stops there for a few minutes, by Tonda's grave, remembering vaguely how they had to bury their friend here one winter's day.

He stands there thinking of the dead man . . . and suddenly, so unexpectedly that his heart misses a beat, he hears a hoarse croak. There is a large raven perched motionless on a stunted pine at the edge of the Waste Ground. It is looking at Krabat, and the boy sees with horror that it too has no left eye.

Now Krabat knows where he stands, and wasting no time, he begins to run, running away as fast as his feet will carry him, going upstream along the Black Water.

When he first stops to get his breath back, a viper comes wriggling through the heather, rears up, hissing, and looks at him—it has only one eye. The fox watching him from the undergrowth is one-eyed too.

Krabat runs, stops for breath, runs on, stops again. Toward evening he comes to the far side of the fen. When he comes out into the open, so he hopes, he will be out of the Master's reach. Quickly, he dips his hands in the water, splashes his forehead and temples. Then, tucking in his shirt, which had come adrift as he ran, he tightens his belt, takes the last few steps—and freezes with horror.

Instead of coming out on the open moor, as he ex-

pected, he finds himself in a clearing, and in the middle of this clearing, in the peaceful evening light, stands the mill. The Master is waiting for him at the door of the house.

"Why, if it isn't Krabat!" There is mockery in his voice. "I was just about to send someone out to search for you!"

Krabat is furious. He cannot understand what went wrong. He runs away again, early in the morning this time, before daybreak, in the opposite direction, out of the wood, over fields and meadows, through villages and hamlets. He leaps over watercourses, he wades through a bog, he never stops to rest. He ignores ravens, vipers, foxes; he does not glance at fish or cat, chicken or drake. "They can have one eye or two, or be stone blind for all I care!" he thinks. "I won't be led astray this time!"

All the same, at the end of the long day he is standing outside the mill in the fen of Kosel again. This time the miller's men are there to welcome him back, Lyshko with malicious remarks, the others silently and with sympathy in their eyes. Krabat is near despair. He knows it would be best to give up, but he refuses to admit it. He tries again, a third time, that very night.

It is not difficult to slip away from the mill . . . now he will guide himself by the North Star! What does it matter if he stumbles and gets scratched and bruised in the dark? No one sees him, no one can cast any spell on him, and that is the main thing.

Not far away, an owl hoots, and then another bird flits past. Soon after that he spots an old eagle owl in the starlight; it is sitting on a branch, within his reach, and watching him—with its right eye. Its left eye is missing.

Krabat runs on, falling over roots, stumbling into a ditch. He is not much surprised, when day breaks, to find himself standing outside the mill for the third time.

All is still quiet indoors at this hour, but for the sound of Juro at work in the kitchen, busy making up the fire. Hearing him, Krabat goes in.

"You were right, Juro. No one can run away from here."

Juro gives him something to drink. "You'd better go and wash, Krabat," he says. He helps Krabat off with his wet, muddy, bloodstained shirt, fills a pitcher of water, and then seriously and without his usual foolish grin, he says, "You couldn't do it on your own, Krabat . . . but perhaps it might be done by two. Suppose we both try another time?"

Krabat was awakened by the sound of the miller's men coming upstairs to bed. He still had the taste of the sausage in his mouth; he could not have slept long, even though he had lived through two days and two nights in his dream.

The next morning he happened to be alone with Juro for a moment or two.

"I dreamed of you, Juro," said Krabat. "You suggested something to me in my dream."

"I did?" said Juro. "Well, it must have been nonsense, Krabat, and you'd better just forget about it!"

5 · THE MAN WITH THE PLUMED HAT

THE MILL in the fen of Kosel had seven sets of millstones. Six sets were always in use, and the seventh never; they called those millstones the Dead Stones. They stood right at the back of the grinding room. At first Krabat thought part of the cogwheel must be broken, or the main shaft was stuck, or some other part of the machinery damaged, until one morning, as he was sweeping the place out, he found a little flour lying on the floorboards around the chute that led down to the meal bin under the Dead Stones. On closer inspection, he found traces of fresh flour in the meal bin too, as if it had not been knocked out well enough after the work was done.

Had the Dead Stones been grinding grain last night? If so, it must have been done in secret, while everyone was asleep . . . or were they not all sleeping as soundly as Krabat himself last night?

He remembered that the miller's men had turned up for breakfast looking pale and hollow-eyed that day, and many of them were yawning, which struck him as suspicious now. Impelled by curiosity, he climbed the wooden steps up to the bin floor, where the grain was tipped from its sacks into the funnel-shaped hopper, from which it ran over the feed shoe and so down between the millstones. As the men tipped it in, a few grains were bound to be spilled; only it was not grain of any kind lying there under the hopper, as Krabat expected. The things lying around the bin floor looked like pebbles at first sight; a second glance showed Krabat that they were teeth—teeth and splinters of bone.

Horrified, the boy opened his mouth to scream, but he could not utter a sound.

Suddenly Tonda was there, behind him. Krabat had not heard him coming. He took the boy's hand.

"What are you after up here, Krabat?" he asked. "Come along down, before the Master catches you, and forget what you have seen here, do you hear me, Krabat? Forget it!"

Then he led Krabat down the steps, and no sooner did the boy feel the boards of the grinding-room floor under his feet than all he had seen that morning was wiped clean out of his mind.

During the second half of February, a severe frost set in. The miller's men had to break the ice outside the sluice every morning. Overnight, while the wheel stood still, the water would freeze in the grooves of the paddles, forming thick crusts of ice, which had to be hacked away before the machinery could be started up.

Most dangerous of all was the ice that formed in the tailrace below the mill wheel. To keep it from damaging the wheel two men had to climb down from time to time and hack it out, a job that none of them was particularly keen to do. Tonda made sure that no one shirked it, but

when it was Krabat's turn the head journeyman climbed
down into the tailrace himself, saying it was no work for a
boy who might hurt himself doing it.

The others made no objection, except for Kito, who
grumbled as usual, and Lyshko, who said, "Anyone might
hurt himself if he didn't look out!"

Whether by chance or not, stupid Juro happened to be
passing just then with a bucket full of pig swill in each
hand. As he came past Lyshko he stumbled and splashed
him with the pig swill from head to foot. Lyshko swore,
and Juro, wringing his hands, assured him he could kick
himself for being so clumsy.

"Just think how you'll smell for the next few days!" said
he. "And it's all my fault . . . oh dear, Lyshko, don't be
cross with me, please don't! I feel so sorry for the poor
pigs too!"

These days Krabat often went out felling trees in the
wood, with Tonda and some of the others. As they set off
in their sleigh, well wrapped up, hot oatmeal inside them,
their fur caps crammed down on their foreheads, he felt
so good in spite of the bitter cold that he envied no one in
the world.

The trees they felled had their branches lopped on the
spot, were stripped of their bark, cut to the right length,
and stacked up loosely, with crossbars running between
each layer to let the air in between the trunks, before they
were taken to the mill next winter to be made into beams
or sawn up for planks and boards.

So the weeks passed by, and nothing much changed in
Krabat's daily life. He noticed a good many things that
made him stop to think. For a start, it was odd that no

customers ever came to the mill. Were the local farmers avoiding it? Yet the millstones ground every day, and grain was always being poured into the hoppers—barley and oats and buckwheat.

Did the flour that was poured from the meal bins into sacks by day turn back into grain overnight? It seemed perfectly possible, Krabat thought.

At the end of the first week in March the weather changed. A west wind sprang up, driving gray clouds across the sky. "There'll be snow," muttered Kito. "I can feel it in my bones!" And it did snow a little, large, watery flakes, before the first raindrops came splashing down and the snow turned to a downpour.

"I tell you what," said Andrush to Kito. "You'd better keep a tree frog to tell you what the weather will be—there's no relying on your bones these days!"

It rained cats and dogs, the rain poured down in torrents, whipped along by the wind, melting snow and ice, and making the millstream rise alarmingly. The men had to go out in the rain to close the sluice and shore it up with props.

Would the sluice gate hold against the rising water?

"If it goes on like this we'll all be drowned along with the mill before three days are up!" thought Krabat.

On the evening of the sixth day the rain stopped, there was a break in the blanket of clouds, and for a few moments the rays of the setting sun shone through the dark, dripping wood.

The next night Krabat had a frightening dream. Fire had broken out in the mill. The miller's men jumped up from their straw mattresses and clattered downstairs, but

Krabat himself lay on his bed like a log of wood, unable to move from the spot.

Flames were already crackling in the rafters, and the first sparks were showering down on his face, when he woke with a yell.

He rubbed his eyes and yawned, looking around him. All of a sudden he froze, unable to believe his eyes. Where were the miller's men?

Their beds were empty, deserted; they seemed to have left in a hurry, since the blankets were hastily pushed back and the sheets crumpled. Here was a jacket on the floor, there a cap, a muffler, a belt—all clearly visible in the reflection of a red light flickering outside the gable window . . .

Was the mill really on fire?

Wide awake now, Krabat flung the window open. Leaning out, he saw a cart standing outside the mill. It was heavily laden, a canvas cover, dark with the rain, was stretched tightly over it, and a team of six horses, every one of them as black as coal, was harnessed to it. Someone was sitting on the box, his collar pulled up high, his hat well down over his forehead, and all his clothes were black as night too. Only the feather he wore in his hat was bright red. It was wavering in the wind like a flame flickering, now blown upward, glowing bright, now drooping as if it would go out. It was bright enough to light up the whole front yard of the mill.

The miller's men were hurrying back and forth between the house and the covered cart, unloading sacks, dragging them into the mill, running out again. They worked in complete silence and feverish haste. Not a shout nor a curse could be heard, only the panting of the men, and now and then a snap as the driver cracked his whip right above their heads, so that they could feel the wind of it. That spurred them on to redouble their efforts. Even the Master was hard at work, though he usually never did a hand's turn in the mill, never lifted his little finger. But tonight he was working with the rest, competing with his men as if he were being paid for it.

Once he stopped work for a moment and vanished into the darkness; not for a rest, as Krabat suspected, but to run to the millstream, move away the props and open the sluice.

The water shot into the millrace, came rushing along and poured over into the tailrace, surging and slapping. With a creaking sound, the wheel began to turn; it was some time before it really got going, but then it went smoothly around. And now the millstones ought to start grinding, with a hollow groaning noise, but there was only one set of stones working, and that one set of stones worked with an unfamiliar sound. Krabat thought it seemed to come right from the back of the mill, a noisy clatter and thud, accompanied by an ugly squealing sound which soon turned to a howl that tormented the listener's ears.

Krabat remembered the Dead Stones, and his flesh began to creep.

Meanwhile work was still going on down below. The covered cart was unloaded, and the miller's men had a break—but not for long. The work went on again, though this time they were carrying the sacks back from the house to the cart. Whatever those sacks had contained, it was now ground and was being brought back.

Krabat meant to count the sacks, but he nodded off to sleep in the middle. At first cockcrow the rumble of cart-wheels awakened him, and he was just in time to see the stranger drive away over the wet meadow, cracking his whip, going toward the wood—and strange to say, heavily laden as it was, the cart left no tracks behind it in the grass.

A moment later the sluice was closed and the mill wheel ran down. Krabat jumped back into bed and pulled the covers up over his head. The miller's men came staggering upstairs, tired to death. They lay down on their beds in silence, only Kito muttering something about "these accursed nights of new moon" and "a fiendish job."

In the morning Krabat was so tired he could hardly get up. His head was throbbing, and he had a queasy feeling in his stomach. At breakfast he looked at the miller's men; they were sleepy and bleary-eyed and surly as they ate their oatmeal. Even Andrush was disinclined to make jokes; he stared gloomily at his plate and did not say a word.

After breakfast Tonda took the boy aside.

"Did you have a bad night?"

"I—I'm not sure," said Krabat. "I didn't have to work, I was just watching. But what about you? Why didn't you wake me when the stranger came? I suppose you wanted to keep it secret from me—like all the other things that go on at this mill, and I'm not to know about them! But I'm not deaf or blind, you know, and I'm no fool either, not by any means!"

"No one said you were!" protested Tonda.

"But that's the way you all act!" cried Krabat. "You're

playing some kind of game with me! Why don't you stop it?"

"All in good time," said Tonda quietly. "You'll learn all about this mill and its Master soon enough. The day and the hour are nearer than you know. Be patient until then."

6 · THE RAVENS' PERCH

ARLY on Good Friday evening there was a pale, bloated moon hanging in the sky above the fen of Kosel. The miller's men were sitting together in the servants' hall, while Krabat, worn out, was lying on his bed trying to get to sleep. They had had to work on Good Friday too. He felt thankful it was evening at last, and he could get some rest . . .

All of a sudden he heard his name called, just as it was in the dream he had in the smithy at Petershain, only now he knew the hoarse voice that seemed to come out of thin air.

He sat up and listened, and the voice called again. "Krabat!" Reaching for his clothes, he got dressed.

When he was ready, the Master called him for the third time.

Krabat made haste, groped his way to the attic door and opened it. Light shone up from below. Down in the hall he heard voices, and the clatter of wooden clogs. Feeling uneasy, he hesitated, holding his breath—but then he pulled himself together and ran downstairs, three steps at a time.

The eleven journeymen were standing at the end of the hall. The door to the Black Room stood open, and the Master was sitting behind the table. Just as on the day of Krabat's arrival, the thick, leather-bound book was lying in front of him, and there was the skull too, with the red candle burning in it. The only difference was that the Master was not so pale in the face now.

"Come closer, Krabat!" he said.

The boy came forward, to the threshold of the Black Room. He did not feel tired now, nor did he notice his dizziness or the throbbing of his heart anymore.

The Master looked him over. Then, raising his left hand, he turned to the journeymen standing in the hall.

"Up on your perch!"

Croaking and flapping their wings, eleven ravens flew past Krabat and through the door of the room. When he looked around, the miller's men had disappeared. The ravens settled on a perch at the far end of the room, in the left corner, and sat there looking at him.

The Master rose, and his shadow fell on the boy.

"You have been at this mill for a quarter of a year now, Krabat," said he. "Your trial period is over, and you are no longer an ordinary apprentice—from now on you will be my pupil."

With these words he went up to Krabat and touched the boy's left shoulder with his own left hand. A shiver ran through Krabat, he felt himself begin to shrink, his body became smaller and smaller, he grew raven's feathers, a beak and claws. There he crouched in the doorway, at the Master's feet, not daring to look up.

The Master looked down at him for a while, then clapped his hands and cried, "Up on your perch!" Krabat —the raven Krabat—obediently spread his wings and rose into the air. Flapping awkwardly, he crossed the room, flew around the table, brushing against the book and the skull, and then settled beside the other ravens, clinging tight to the perch.

"You must know that you are in a Black School, Krabat," the Master told him. "You will not learn reading and writing and arithmetic here—you will learn the Art of Arts. The book chained to the table is the Book of Necromancy, which teaches how to conjure up spirits. As you see, it has black pages, and the words are white. It contains all the magic spells in the world. I alone may read them, because I am the Master here. But you—you, Krabat, and my other pupils—you are forbidden to read the Book, remember that! And no going behind my back, or it will be the worse for you! Do you understand that, Krabat?"

"Yes, I understand," croaked the boy, surprised to find he could still speak at all—in a hoarse voice, to be sure, but quite clearly and easily.

Krabat had heard whispered tales of such Black Schools before. There were said to be several of them in Lusatia, but he had always supposed those were just old wives' tales, such as women will tell while they sit and spin. Now he was a pupil in a Black School himself, though it appeared to be an ordinary mill! Yet it seemed that those who lived nearby, at least, said there was something strange about the place, or why did the people of the fen of Kosel keep away?

The boy had no time to pursue his thoughts, for the Master, sitting down at the table again, was beginning to read an extract from the Book of Necromancy. He read slowly, in a singsong voice, rocking stiffly back and forth from his hips as he did so.

"This is the way to make a well run dry, so that it will give no water from one day to the next," he read out. "First get four pegs of birch wood, dried over the stove, each two and a half spans long, as broad as your thumb, and sharpened to a three-cornered point at one end. Next you must place your pegs of wood around the well by night, between twelve and one, driving each into the ground seven feet from the well, every one at a different point of the compass, beginning with midnight and ending with evening. Third and lastly, when you have done all this, saying no word, you must walk around the well three times and speak the words written here . . ."

Then the Master read out a magic spell, a sequence of incomprehensible words, fair-sounding, all of them, and yet there was a dark undertone, suggesting something evil, that lingered in the boy's ears, even when the Master began again after a brief pause.

"This is the way to make a well run dry . . ."

He read the passage from the Book and the magic spell three times in all, always in the same singsong voice, rocking back and forth from the waist. After the third time he closed the book. He waited in silence for a while, and then turned to the ravens.

"Now I have taught you a new piece of the Secret Arts," said he, in his normal voice. "Let's hear how much you remember of it. You there—begin!"

He pointed to one of the ravens, and told him to repeat the passage and the magic spell.

"This is the way . . . to make a well run dry . . . so that . . . so that it will give no water from one day to the next . . ."

The miller picked on first one raven, then another, and questioned each one. He did not call any of the twelve by name, but Krabat could tell them apart by the way they spoke. Even when he was a raven, Tonda's voice was calm and deliberate, Kito spoke with an unmistakably peevish tone and Andrush was as quick with his beak as with his tongue, while Juro, when it was his turn to repeat the spell, had great difficulty and kept getting stuck; in short, there was not one of them whom Krabat could not identify.

"This is the way to make a well run dry . . ."

Again and again they repeated the passage from the Book of Necromancy and the magic spell, some fluently, some hesitantly, a fifth time, a ninth, an eleventh.

"Now you!" The Master turned to Krabat.

The boy began to tremble. He stammered, "This is the way . . . is the way to make a . . . a well . . ."

Here he broke off, struck dumb. With the best will in the world, he could not remember how it went on. Would the Master punish him?

The Master did not seem at all angry.

"You'd better pay more attention to the words than the voices another time, Krabat," he said. "Remember, no one is forced to learn in this school! If you master the passages I read you from the Book, it will be to your advantage; if not, it hurts no one but yourself!"

So saying, he finished the lesson. The door opened and the ravens flew out. Back in the hall, they returned to human form; Krabat too was changed back, he did not know how or by whom, and as he made his way up to the attic behind the miller's men, he felt as though he had dreamed some strange, confusing dream.

7 · THE SIGN OF THE SECRET BROTHERHOOD

HE NEXT day, which was Easter Eve, the miller's men did not have to work. Most of them seized their chance to go back to bed after breakfast. "You'd better go upstairs and get some sleep too," Tonda told Krabat. "You'll be needing it."

"Why?"

"You'll find out why. Go and lie down now, and try to sleep as long as you can."

"All right, I'm going!" muttered Krabat. "Sorry I asked!"

Up in the attic, someone had hung a piece of cloth over the gable window, which was a good idea; it made it easier to get to sleep. Krabat settled down on his right side, his back to the window, his head buried in his arms. He lay there sleeping until Juro came to wake him.

"Get up, Krabat—the food's on the table."

"Why, is it midday already?"

Laughing, Juro pulled the cloth back from the window.

"Midday! That's a good one!" said he. "The sun will soon be sinking out there, sleepyhead!"

The miller's men had their dinner and supper rolled into one that day. It was a good, plentiful meal, almost a feast.

"Eat all you can!" Tonda told the men. "It will have to last you some time, as you know."

After their meal, as night fell before the dawn of Easter Day, the Master came to the servants' hall where they were sitting and sent out his men "to bring back the sign."

They formed a circle around him, and he began to count them out, as children do playing tag or hide-and-seek. Reciting some words that had a strange, menacing sound, the Master counted first from right to left, then from left to right. The first time Stashko was counted out, and the second time it was Andrush. The two of them left the circle in silence and went away, while the Master began to count again. Next time it was Merten and Hanzo who had to go, and then Lyshko and Petar. Finally, only Krabat and Tonda were left.

For the last time the Master repeated the strange, ominous words, slowly and solemnly, then dismissed them both with a gesture and turned away.

Tonda signed to Krabat to follow him, and in silence they too left the mill and went out to the woodshed together.

"Wait here a moment!" Tonda fetched two blankets from the shed and gave one of them to Krabat. Then he set off along the path to Schwarzkollm, past the millpond and through the fen.

As they entered the wood the last of the daylight went. Krabat tried hard to keep close to Tonda, and it occurred to him that he had walked this way once before, though in the opposite direction and on his own, in wintertime.

Could that really be little more than three months ago? It seemed incredible!

"There's Schwarzkollm," said Tonda after a while.

They saw the lights of the village shining between the tree trunks, but they themselves bore right, out onto the open moor. The path was dry and sandy here, and led past a few stunted trees, shrubs and bushes. The sky was high and wide, bright with starlight.

"Where are we going?" Krabat asked.

"To Dead Man's Cross," said the head journeyman.

A little later they caught sight of a fire burning on the moor, flickering at the bottom of a sandy hollow. Who could have lit it?

"Not shepherds, for certain," said Krabat to himself, "not so early in the year. It must be gypsies, or a traveling tinker with his wares."

Tonda had stopped. "They're at Dead Man's Cross before us—let's go to Baumel's End."

He turned, without a word of explanation, and they had to make their way back to the wood by the same path. Then they turned right, along a footpath that led them past the village of Schwarzkollm and joined a road on the other side of it, leading to the outskirts of the wood opposite.

"It's not far," said Tonda.

By now the moon had risen, and was giving them light. They followed the road to the next bend, where a wooden cross as tall as a man stood in the shadow of the pines. It was plain and very weather-beaten, and it bore no inscription.

"This is Baumel's End," said Tonda. "Many years ago a man called Baumel lost his life here, while he was cutting wood, they say, though no one knows now exactly how it happened."

"What about us?" asked Krabat. "Why are we here?"

"We're here because the Master says so," said Tonda. "All twelve of us have to spend the night before Easter out of doors, in couples, each couple at a spot where someone met with a violent death."

"And what do we do now?" asked Krabat.

"We light a fire," said Tonda. "Then we keep watch under this cross until dawn, and at the break of day we must mark each other with the sign."

They kept the fire low purposely, so as not to arouse any attention over in Schwarzkollm. Each wrapped in his blanket, they sat and kept watch under the wooden cross. Now and then Tonda asked the boy if he was cold, or told him to put a few of the dry branches they had picked up in the wood on the fire. As time went by, he was increasingly silent. Krabat tried to get a conversation going himself.

"Tonda."

"What is it?"

"Is the Black School always like that? With the Master reading something from the Book and then saying, 'Let's see how much you remember . . .'?"

"Yes," said Tonda.

"I don't see how you can learn magic that way."

"Well, you can," said Tonda.

"Do you think I annoyed the Master because I wasn't attending?"

"No."

"I'll do better in the future—I'll make sure to notice everything! Do you think I'll manage it?"

"Yes," said Tonda.

He did not seem to want to talk to Krabat very much. He sat there upright, his back against the cross, gazing into the distance, past the village, to the moonlit moor, and after this conversation he said nothing else at all. When Krabat spoke his name softly, he did not reply; a dead man could not have been quieter or gazed more fixedly into space.

As time went by, the boy began to feel there was something uncanny about the way Tonda was acting. He remembered hearing that some folk knew the art of "going out of themselves," slipping out of the body like a butterfly emerging from a chrysalis, and leaving it behind, an empty shell, while their true selves went their own invisible way, on secret paths, to a secret goal. Had Tonda "gone out of himself"? Was it possible that while he sat here by the fire, he was really somewhere quite different?

"I must keep awake," Krabat told himself.

He propped himself first on his right elbow, then on his left; he made sure the fire kept burning steadily, he occupied himself breaking up the branches into handy lengths and arranging them in neat little piles. And so the hours went by. The stars passed over the sky, the shadows of the trees and houses moved away under the moon, slowly changing their shape.

Quite suddenly, or so it seemed, Tonda came back to life. Leaning over to Krabat, he pointed to the countryside around them.

"The bells—do you hear them?"

The church bells had been silent since Maundy Thursday; now, as Easter came in, they began to ring again, all over the country. Their peals floated across the fields to

Schwarzkollm from the nearby village churches, muffled, only a faint noise, like the humming of a swarm of bees— yet the moor, the village, the fields and the meadows were filled with the sound to the farthest rim of the hills.

At almost the same moment as the distant bells rang out, a girl's voice was raised in song in Schwarzkollm village. She was singing an old Easter hymn of rejoicing. Krabat knew the tune, he used to sing it in church himself as a child, but he felt as if he were hearing it for the first time.

> Christ is risen!
> Christ is risen!
> Hallelujah, hallelujah!

Then a group of twelve or fifteen more girls joined in, singing the rest of the verse in chorus. The girl who led the choir began the next verse, and so they went on, first a solo, then all together, one hymn after another.

Krabat had heard it all before; on the morning of Easter Day at home the girls used to go up and down the village street singing, from midnight until dawn. They walked close together, side by side, in groups of three or four, and one of them, he knew, would lead the singing, the one with the purest and sweetest voice of all. She walked in the front row and sang the solo part.

The bells rang from afar, the girls sang, and Krabat, sitting by the fire under the wooden cross, held his breath. He listened and listened to the music coming from the village, as if spellbound.

Tonda put a branch on the fire.

"I loved a girl once," said he. "Vorshula was her name.

She has been lying in the graveyard of Seidewinkel six months now; it was little luck I brought her. Krabat, remember that none of us at the mill brings a girl luck! I don't know why that is, and I don't want to alarm you, but Krabat, if ever you love a girl, beware of showing it! Take care the Master doesn't find out, or Lyshko, who's always carrying tales to him."

"Why—did the Master and Lyshko have anything to do with the death of the girl you loved?" asked Krabat.

"I do not know," said Tonda. "All I know is that Vorshula would be alive today if I had kept her name to myself, but I only found that out too late. But you, Krabat —you know now, and you know in time! If ever you love a girl, don't tell her name in the mill! Let nothing in the world get it out of you! Tell no one, do you hear, no one! Not awake, nor in your sleep, or it will bring bad luck to both of you!"

"Never fear!" said Krabat. "I've no time for girls, and I can't see myself changing my mind about that!"

At daybreak the bells and the singing in the village fell silent. Tonda cut two splinters of wood from the cross with his knife. They put the splinters in the embers of their fire and charred the ends.

"Do you know what a pentagram is?" asked Tonda.

"No," said Krabat.

"Watch me, then."

With the tip of his finger Tonda drew a figure in the sand, a five-pointed star formed of five straight lines, each intersecting two others so that the whole figure could be drawn in a single movement.

"This is the sign," said Tonda. "Now draw it yourself."

"It can't be difficult," said the boy. "First you did this . . . then this . . . then this . . ."

At his third attempt Krabat succeeded in drawing the pentagram in the sand correctly.

"Good," said Tonda, putting one of the wooden splinters into his hand. "Now kneel by the fire, reach across the embers, and draw the sign on my forehead, and I'll tell you what you have to say."

Krabat did as the head journeyman told him, and as they drew the pentagram on each other's foreheads, he repeated the words slowly:

> I mark you, brother,
> with wood from the cross.
> I mark you
> with the sign of
> the Secret Brotherhood.

Then they gave each other the Easter kiss on the left cheek, raked sand over their fire, scattered the remaining firewood, and set off for home.

Tonda took the path through the fields again, skirting around the village. He was making for the wood, which was shrouded in morning mist, when they saw the outlines of shadowy figures appear before them in the halflight of dawn. The village girls were coming toward them, silently, in a long file, dark shawls around their heads and shoulders, and each with an earthen pitcher in her hand.

"Come!" said Tonda softly to Krabat. "They've been to draw the Easter water. We don't want to frighten them."

They drew back into the shadow of the nearest hedge and let the girls go by.

The Easter water, as Krabat knew, must be drawn from a spring before sunrise on Easter morning. It must be drawn in silence, and in silence it must be carried home, and if you washed in it you would have beauty and good luck for a whole year—or so the girls used to say.

Moreover, if you carried the Easter water home to the village without ever looking around, you might meet your future lover—so the girls said, but who knew what to think of that?

8 · REMEMBER I AM THE MASTER

HE MASTER had fixed a yoke outside the open door of the house; both ends were nailed to the door frame at shoulder height. As the men came back they had to pass under it, one by one, saying, "I bow beneath the yoke of the Secret Brotherhood."

The Master was waiting for them in the hall, and he gave each man a blow on the right cheek, with the words, "Remember you are my pupil!" Then he struck them on the left cheek, adding, "Remember I am the Master!" After that the men had to bow low to the miller three times, promising, "I will obey you in all things, Master, now and forever."

Tonda and Krabat met with the same reception. The boy did not yet realize that he was now the Master's property, delivered up to him utterly, body and soul, for life or death. He joined the other men, who were standing at the end of the passage, as if they were waiting for their breakfast. They all had the sign of the pentagram drawn on their foreheads, like Tonda and Krabat himself.

Petar and Lyshko were not back yet, but they soon appeared at the door too, and after they had bowed under the yoke, taken their blows on the cheeks and made their promises, the mill began to go around.

"To work!" cried the Master to his men. "Off with you!"

At that the miller's men threw off their coats. They ran to the grinding room, rolling up their sleeves as they went, dragged up sacks of grain and set to work, while the Master kept them hard at it, shouting and gesticulating impatiently. .

"And this is supposed to be Easter Sunday!" thought Krabat. "Not a wink of sleep all night, no breakfast—and we have to work twice as hard as usual!"

Even Tonda ran out of breath at last and began to sweat. They were all sweating freely that morning; the perspiration dripped from their foreheads and temples, ran down their necks, poured down their backs so that their shirts were sticking to them.

"How much longer is this going on?" Krabat wondered.

Whenever he looked, he saw set, grim faces. They were all grunting and groaning, hot and damp with perspiration as they were. And the pentagrams on their foreheads were blurring, dissolving in their sweat, and gradually disappearing.

. Then something quite unexpected happened. Krabat, shouldering a sack of wheat, was struggling up the steps to the bin floor. It took the very last of his strength and every scrap of will power he had. He was just about to stumble and collapse under his burden—when suddenly all his troubles were over. The pain in his legs was gone, his backache had disappeared, and his breathing came easily.

"Tonda!" he cried. "Look at this!"

He was up on the bin floor with one bound, then, tipping the sack off his shoulder, he grabbed it by both ends, and before emptying it into the hopper he brandished it in the air with shouts of triumph, as easily as if it were full of feathers instead of grain.

It was as if the miller's men had been transformed by magic. They stretched their arms, laughed, and slapped their thighs. Even the sour-faced Kito was no exception.

Krabat was hurrying off to the granary to fetch the next sack, but the head journeyman cried, "Stop! That'll do!" They let the wheat run through the mill, and then Tonda stopped the machinery. "That's it for today!" said he.

With a final creak and clatter the mill wheel ran down, and they knocked the flour out of the meal bins.

"And now to make merry, brothers!" shouted Stashko.

All of a sudden there were big pitchers of wine, and Juro was bringing in dishes of Easter cakes, sweet and golden brown, fried in lard and filled with curds or plum jam.

"Fall to, brothers! Eat them up, and don't forget the wine!"

They ate and drank and made merry, and later Andrush began to sing, loud and boisterously. They washed down their cakes with red wine, and then formed a circle, linked arms, and stamped their feet in time to the song.

> The miller, he sits
> At the millhouse door,
> Clackety, clickety,
> Clack!
> Spies as fine a young fellow,
> As ever you saw,

> Clackety, clickety,
> As ever you saw!
> Clackety, clickety,
> Clack!

The miller's men sang the "Clackety, clickety" in chorus; then Hanzo started the next verse, and so they went on, singing in turn and dancing in a ring, first to the right, then to the left, into the middle and out again.

Krabat's turn came last of all, since he was only the apprentice. He shut his eyes and sang the last verse of the song.

> This fine young fellow,
> No fool was he,
> Clackety, clickety,
> Clack!
> He struck the miller,
> Down on his knee,
> Clackety, clickety,
> Down on his knee!
> Clackety, clickety,
> Clack!

They stopped dancing and fell to drinking again. Kubo, who was usually so quiet, took the boy aside and patted him on the back.

"You have a good voice, Krabat. You ought to be singing in a choir!" said he.

"Who, me?" asked Krabat. It was only now Kubo mentioned it that he realized he could sing again—in a deeper voice than before, to be sure, but a voice that was firm and clear. The rasp in his throat that had been bothering him since the beginning of last winter was quite gone.

On Easter Monday the miller's men went back to work as usual. Everything was back to normal—except that Krabat no longer had to toil so hard. He could easily do whatever the Master told him now. It seemed that the days when he dropped on to his bed half dead with exhaustion every evening were gone forever.

Krabat was heartily thankful for it, and he could guess how it had happened. When he and Tonda were next alone together he asked his friend.

"Yes, you're right," said Tonda. "So long as we carry the sign of the pentagram on our foreheads we have to work like slaves—until the moment when the last of us has washed it away in the sweat of his brow. In return, our work will be easy all the year, as long as we do it between dawn and dusk."

"What about other times?" asked Krabat. "After dark, I mean."

"Not then," said Tonda. "We have to manage as best we can after dark! But set your mind at rest, Krabat. For one thing, we don't have to leave our beds to work so very often, and for another, well, it's bearable when it happens!"

They never mentioned the night before Easter again, or Tonda's grief for the girl he loved; they did not even allude to it. Yet Krabat thought he knew where Tonda had been while he sat by the fire like a dead man, staring into the distance. And whenever Krabat thought of Vorshula and her story, the singer of Schwarzkollm, the girl who led the choir, came into his mind—or rather her voice as he had heard it floating across the fields from the village at midnight. This seemed strange to him; he would have liked to forget that voice, yet he found it was impossible.

Once a week, on Fridays, the miller's men assembled outside the Black Room after supper, turned themselves into ravens—Krabat soon learned the trick of it—and settled on their perch. Every Friday the Master read them a passage from the Book of Necromancy; he read it three times in all, and they had to repeat it after him, though the Master himself did not care what or how much of it they remembered.

Krabat was eager to memorize all the Master taught them: storm spells and charms to make hail, the casting of magic bullets and the way to use them, invisibility, the art of going out of one's body, and many other things. While he was working by day, and before he fell asleep at night, he repeated the instructions and the words of the spells from the Book over and over again, so as to stamp them on his memory.

For by now Krabat had realized one thing: a man who knew the Art of Arts had power over other men, and to have power—as much as the Master had, if not more—struck him as a fine thing to aim for. It was to achieve that aim that he was studying and studying and studying.

One night in the second week after Easter the miller's men were called from their beds. The Master was standing at the attic door with a light in his hand.

"There's work to be done!" he cried. "The Goodman is coming—hurry up, make haste!"

In the rush, Krabat could not find his shoes, so he followed the others out of the mill barefoot. There was a new moon; the night was so dark that the miller's men could not see an inch in front of them. In the crush, someone wearing wooden clogs trod on Krabat's toes.

"Hey!" cried the boy. "Watch out, you clumsy oaf!"

A hand was put over his mouth. "Ssh!" Tonda whispered.

Then Krabat realized that not one of the miller's men had spoken a word since the Master woke them. And they did not utter a sound all the rest of that night, nor did Krabat himself.

He could guess what kind of work lay ahead, and soon enough the stranger with the flickering plume in his hat came rattling up in his cart. The men fell upon it, tore off the dark canvas cover, and began dragging sacks into the mill—to the Dead Stones at the far end of the grinding room.

Everything happened just as it had four weeks ago, when Krabat watched the others through the gable window, only this time the Master swung himself up by the stranger's side on the box. Today it was he who cracked the whip, right above their heads, so that the men ducked as they felt it whistle past.

Krabat had almost forgotten what hard work it was to carry a full sack, and how soon you were out of breath.

"Remember that you are my pupil!"

Those were the Master's words, and the longer Krabat thought about them, the less he liked the sound of them.

The whip cracked, the men ran back and forth, the mill wheel went around and the house was filled with the clatter and squeal of the Dead Stones. What was in those sacks? Krabat glanced into the hopper, but he could not make much out in the dim light of the lantern swaying from the ceiling. Was he tipping clods of dirt, or pine cones, into the hopper, or maybe round stones encrusted with mud . . . ?

The boy had no time to take a closer look; Lyshko came up with the next sack, panting, and elbowed Krabat aside.

Michal and Merten had taken up their positions by the meal bin; they refilled the empty sacks with whatever it was that had been ground, and tied them up. Again, everything happened just as before. At first cockcrow the cart was loaded up again, the cover pulled over it and fastened. The stranger reached for his whip, and off he went with his cart, so fast that the Master only just had time to jump down without breaking his neck.

"Come with me!" said Tonda to Krabat.

While the others went into the house the two of them went up to the millrace to shut the sluice. They heard the mill wheel run down below them, and all was quiet, but for the rooster crowing and the hens clucking.

"Does he often come?" asked Krabat, jerking his head in the direction in which the cart had disappeared into the morning mist.

"Every night of new moon," said Tonda.

"Do you know who he is?"

"Only the Master knows that. He calls him the Goodman—and he is afraid of him."

They walked slowly back to the mill through the dewy meadows.

"There's one thing I don't understand," said Krabat, before they entered the house. "Last time the stranger came the Master was working too. Why not today?"

"Last time he had to help us to make up the dozen," said the head journeyman. "But since Easter the numbers of the Black School have been made up, so now he can afford to spend the nights of new moon cracking the whip!"

9 · THE OX DEALER FROM KAMENZ

SOMETIMES the Master sent his men out on errands, in pairs or in small groups, to give them a chance to use the arts they learned in the Black School. One morning Tonda went up to Krabat. "I have to go to the Wittichenau cattle market with Andrush today," he said. "The Master says you can go with us if you like."

"Good!" said Krabat. "It'll make a change from all this grinding of grain!"

They took a path through the wood that joined the road beside some houses near the Neudorf village pond. It was a fine, sunny July day. The jays were calling in the branches, they could hear the tapping of a woodpecker, swarms of honey bees and bumble bees filled the wild raspberry bushes with their buzzing.

Krabat noticed that Tonda and Andrush looked as merry as if they were off to the fair. It couldn't be just the fine weather. Andrush, of course, was always a cheerful, good-tempered fellow, but it was unusual to hear Tonda whistling happily to himself. From time to time he cracked his ox whip.

"Are you practising to do that on the way home?" said Krabat.

"What do you mean, on the way home?"

"I thought we were going to Wittichenau to buy an ox?"

"On the contrary!" said Tonda.

Just at that moment Krabat heard a loud "Moo!" behind him, and when he turned around, there was a fine ox standing where Andrush had been a moment before. It had a smooth, reddish-brown coat, and it was looking at him in a friendly way.

"Hey!" said Krabat, rubbing his eyes.

Suddenly Tonda too was gone, and in his place there stood an old Wendish peasant, wearing felt shoes, linen trousers with cross-gartering from ankle to knee, and a smock belted with a cord. He had a greasy fur cap, its brim rubbed bare.

"Hey!" said Krabat again. Then someone tapped him on the shoulder and laughed. When he turned, there was Andrush back again.

"Where did you go, Andrush? And where's that ox—the one that was standing here just now?"

"Moo!" said Andrush in the ox's voice.

"What about Tonda?"

The peasant turned back into Tonda before Krabat's very eyes.

"So that's it!" said the boy.

"Yes, that's it," said Tonda. "Andrush is going to show his paces in the cattle market."

"You mean you're going to sell him?"

"Those are the Master's orders."

"But—but suppose Andrush gets sent to be slaughtered?"

"No fear of that!" Tonda assured him. "Once we sell Andrush as an ox, all we have to do is keep his halter. Then he can turn himself into any shape he likes, any time he likes."

"Suppose we lose the halter?"

"You dare!" cried Andrush. "If you did that I'd have to stay an ox all my life, eating hay and straw—just you get that into your heads, and don't do any such thing!"

Tonda and Krabat created a great sensation in Wittichenau cattle market. Their ox was much admired. All the dealers came hurrying up and surrounded them, and a few of the townsfolk, and some farmers who had already disposed of their pigs and bullocks, joined the crowd. It wasn't every day you saw such a fine fat ox; they all felt they'd like to get their hands on it before anyone else could snap up such a splendid animal from under their noses.

"How much?"

The cattle dealers showered Tonda with questions, shouting at the tops of their voices. Master Krause the butcher, from Hoyerswerda, offered fifteen guilders for Andrush, and lame Leuschner from Koenigsbruck went one better and offered sixteen.

Tonda merely shook his head. "Not good enough," said he.

"Not good enough?" said they. He must be crazy, they assured him. Did he take them for fools?

"Fools or no," said Tonda, "I suppose you gentlemen must know that best yourselves!"

"Very well, then," said Master Krause from Hoyer-swerda. "Eighteen!"

"Eighteen! Why, I'd rather keep him myself!" growled Tonda. He would not let Master Leuschner from Koenigsbruck have him for nineteen guilders either, or young Gustav Neubauer from Senftenberg for twenty.

"The devil take you and your ox, then!" cried Master Krause angrily, and Master Leuschner, tapping his forehead, said, "I'd be a fool to ruin myself. Twenty-two, and that's my last word!"

The bargaining seemed to have reached a deadlock when a fat, shapeless man, puffing like a grampus at every step he took, pushed his way through the crowd. His frog-face with its round goggle eyes was shiny with sweat, he wore a green tailcoat with silver buttons, a showy watch chain over his red satin vest, and there was a fat purse at his belt for all the world to see.

Master Blaschke, the ox dealer from Kamenz, was one of the richest and probably the shrewdest of all the cattle dealers for miles around. Pushing Master Leuschner and young Gustav Neubauer aside, he shouted in his loud, blustering voice, "How in heaven's name did such a thin fellow come by such a fat ox? I'll take him for twenty-five!"

Tonda scratched his ear. "Not good enough, sir," said he.

"Not good enough! Did you ever hear the like of that?" Blaschke took out a big silver snuffbox, snapped open the lid and offered it to Tonda. "Want a pinch?" He let the old Wendish peasant take snuff before he took a pinch himself.

"A-tishoo—that's the right stuff and no mistake!"

"Thankee, sir!"

Blaschke blew his nose on a big checked handkerchief. "The devil take it, then—twenty-seven! Hand him over!"

"Not good enough, sir."

Master Blaschke went scarlet in the face.

"What do you think I am? Twenty-seven guilders for your ox, not a penny more, or my name's not Blaschke of Kamenz!"

"Thirty, sir," said Tonda. "You can have him for thirty."

"It's daylight robbery!" cried Blaschke. "Do you want to ruin me?" He rolled his eyes and wrung his hands. "Have you no heart? Are you blind and deaf to the troubles of a poor fellow trying to make an honest living? Don't be so hard-hearted, old man—let me have your ox for twenty-eight!"

Tonda stood firm.

"Thirty, and that's that! This ox is a fine specimen, worth every penny! You've no notion how hard it is for me to part with him. Why, it couldn't be worse if I was selling my own son!"

Blaschke realized he was getting nowhere, but the ox really was a beautiful animal. Why waste more time with this pigheaded Wend?

"Hand him over, then, in the devil's name!" he cried. "This is my day for being soft-hearted—anyone can just wind me around his little finger! It's a weakness of mine! All because I have a kind heart and I'm good to the poor . . . well, give us your hand on it, then. Done!"

"Done!" said Tonda.

Taking off his cap, he made Blaschke count out the thirty guilders into it, one by one.

"Did you count them too?" asked Blaschke.

"I did."

"Come here, then, my Wendish ox!"

Blaschke took Andrush by the halter and was about to lead him off, but Tonda grasped the fat man's sleeve.

"Well, what is it?" asked Blaschke.

"Why, now," said Tonda, acting embarrassment, "it's a little thing, nothing much . . ."

"Come on, out with it!"

"If you'd be so kind as to leave me that halter, Master Blaschke, I'd be very grateful . . ."

"The halter?"

"As a keepsake," said Tonda. "You must know how hard it is for me to part with my ox, Master Blaschke! I'll give you another halter instead, Master Blaschke, so you can take my poor ox away now he's not mine anymore . . ."

Tonda untied the cord he was wearing as a belt, and Blaschke, shrugging his shoulders, let him exchange it for the ox's halter. Then the dealer went off with Andrush, and he was hardly around the corner before he began to grin broadly. Maybe he *had* paid thirty guilders for Andrush, and that was a pretty steep price, but he could easily sell such a fine ox for double that in Dresden, maybe more.

Tonda and Krabat sat down on the grass in the outskirts of the wood, behind the village pond and the houses, to wait for Andrush. They had bought a piece of bacon and a loaf of bread in Wittichenau, and they ate some of it.

"You were really good!" Krabat told Tonda. "You should have seen yourself—the way you squeezed the money out of that fat fellow! 'Not good enough, sir, not good enough . . . !' A good thing you remembered the halter in time. I'd have clean forgotten it myself!"

"You'll soon learn," Tonda reassured him.

They put a piece of bread and bacon aside for Andrush, wrapping them both in Krabat's smock, and then decided to lie down for a while. Well fed as they were, and tired from their long walk, they fell asleep and slept soundly, until a "Moo!" woke them, and there was Andrush, back in human form and sound in wind and limb, so far as anyone could see.

"Hey there, you two—folks have been known to sleep themselves silly before now! I hope you've at least left me a crust of bread!"

"Bread and bacon too," said Tonda. "Sit down, brother, and eat it up! How did you get on with Blaschke?"

"Why, how do you suppose?" muttered Andrush. "It's no fun to be an ox, I can tell you, and trot across country for miles, breathing in all the dust, especially when you're not used to it! Well, I didn't mind at all when Blaschke turned in at the alehouse in Ossling. He and the innkeeper there are cousins, you see, and they do a lot of business together too. 'Look at that!' cries the innkeeper, when he sees us coming. 'If it isn't my cousin from Kamenz! How are you keeping, then—how are things with you?' 'Not so bad,' says Blaschke, 'not so bad at all, if it wasn't for the thirst this heat gives a man.' 'We'll soon see to that,' says the innkeeper. 'Come along into the taproom! There's plenty of beer in the cellar—even you couldn't finish it inside of seven weeks!' 'How about my ox?' the fat man asks. 'That ox cost me thirty guilders!' 'We'll put him in the stables and he can have all the water and fodder he likes!' Fodder for oxen, he meant, of course . . ."

Andrush speared a big chunk of bacon on his knife and

sniffed at it before stuffing it into his mouth.

"So they put me in the stable," he went on, "and the innkeeper calls for the girl who helps with the horses. 'Here, Kathel,' says he, 'see to this ox—he belongs to my cousin from Kamenz, and we don't want him losing any weight!' 'Very good, sir,' says Kathel, stuffing an armful of hay into my manger right away. That was enough for me; I was tired of being an ox! I didn't think twice about it, I can tell you, I just said in my own voice, in human words, 'You can eat your hay and straw yourself! Roast pork is what I fancy, with cabbage and dumplings, and a mug of good beer!' "

"And then what?" cried Krabat.

"Oh, well," said Andrush, "at that the three of them were so frightened their legs gave way beneath them and down they all plumped! They shouted for help as if they were being roasted alive. I mooed at them again, just to say good-by, and then I turned into a swallow and flew out of the door—cheep-cheep, and I was gone!"

"What about Master Blaschke?"

"The devil take Master Blaschke and his cattle dealing!" Andrush reached for the ox whip and cracked it hard, as if to lend his words force. "I'm glad to be myself again, pockmarks and all!"

"I'm glad of it too," said Tonda. "You played your part well, and I daresay Krabat has learned a lot."

"I have indeed!" cried the boy. "I know what fun it can be to work magic now!"

"Fun?" The head journeyman sounded serious all of a sudden. "Fun? Well, you may be right . . . it can be fun at times!"

10 · MILITARY MUSIC

FOR YEARS the Elector of Saxony had been at war with the King of Sweden for the Polish crown. Now if you must go to war, what you need most of all, after money and guns, is soldiers, and so he had drums beating busily all over the country, and officers at work enlisting men. There were plenty of young fellows ready to join the army, especially at the start of the war; there were others who needed a little persuasion from the recruiting officers, whether in the form of blows or brandy . . . but a man wouldn't balk at that in the service of a glorious regiment, the more so as there was a special bonus payment for every man who could be induced to enlist!

A small party of men, consisting of a lieutenant of the Dresden Foot, a great bear of a corporal, two private soldiers and a drummer who carried his drum on his back like a pack, lost their way in the fen of Kosel one evening. Dusk was already gathering, the Master had been away for three or four days, and the miller's men were in the servants' hall, planning to take things easy for the rest of the day, when there came a knock at the door. Tonda went to answer it. There stood the lieutenant with his men. He was an officer of His Serene Highness the Elector, he barked at Tonda—he had lost his way, and so he had decided to spend the night in this wretched hole of a mill; was that quite clear?

"To be sure, your Worship! There'll be plenty of room in the hayloft!"

"The hayloft?" spluttered the corporal. "The fellow must be off his head! The best bed in the mill for his Worship, by thunder, and devil take you if mine's a bit worse! We're hungry, too. So bring us whatever you have in the kitchen, and some beer or wine, never mind which, so long as there's enough of it—and enough there must be, or I'll break every bone in your body with my own hands! Quick, march, now, and get a move on, plague take you!"

Tonda whistled through his teeth, very briefly, very quietly, but the miller's men in the servants' hall all heard him. When the head journeyman came back into the room with the party of soldiers, it was quite empty.

"Will your lordships please be seated, and the food will come at once!" said Tonda.

While the uninvited guests made themselves at home, loosened their neckcloths and unbuttoned their gaiters, the miller's men were putting their heads together in the kitchen.

"Those pigtailed apes!" cried Andrush. "Who do they think they are?"

He had a plan, and all the others, even Tonda, liked it. Andrush and Stashko quickly prepared a meal, with some help from Michal and Merten: three dishes full of bran and sawdust, mixed to a mush with rancid linseed oil and seasoned with crumbs of tobacco. Juro ran out to the pigsty and came back with two moldy loaves under his arm, and Krabat and Hanzo filled five tankards with brackish water from the rainwater butt in the yard.

When it was all ready Tonda went back to the soldiers and announced that dinner was ready, and if his Worship permitted, he would have it served up. Thereupon he snapped his fingers . . . and that was a special sort of finger-snapping, as was soon to be seen.

First the head journeyman had the three dishes brought in.

"Now here, if it please your lordships, we have noodle soup with beef, chicken and giblets, there's a dish of tripe and kale, and that one is vegetables—white beans and fried onions, with pork crackling . . ."

The lieutenant sniffed the dishes; he was finding it hard to choose.

"This is good food you've brought us! I'll take some of the soup, for a start."

And there was ham and smoked meat too, Tonda told them, pointing to the mouldy bread Juro was bringing in on a plate.

"But there's still something missing—something very important!" the corporal reminded him. "Smoked meat gives you a thirst, and a good thirst must be quenched while it's young, by thunder and lightning and all the plagues of Egypt, it must!"

At a sign from Tonda, Hanzo, Krabat, Petar, Lyshko and Kubo came marching in, each carrying a tankard full of rainwater.

"By your leave, your Worship—your very good health!"

The corporal drank to the lieutenant, then wiped his moustache and hiccuped.

"Not bad, upon my soul! Not at all bad! Home-brewed?"

"No," said Tonda, "it comes from the Rainwater brewery, if it please your Worship!"

It was a merry evening. The soldiers ate and drank enough for ten, and the miller's men were in high spirits—*they* could see what their lordships were really eating, little as the soldiers guessed it themselves!

The water butt was a big one, and the gutters that ran into it provided plenty to drink, enough to fill the tankards time and time again. Gradually the soldiers' faces became flushed. The drummer boy, a lad of Krabat's own age, toppled forward like a sack of flour upon draining his fifth tankard, his head hit the table top with a noise like a kettledrum, and he began to snore. The others went on with the serious business of drinking, and in the midst of their carousing the lieutenant, happening to glance at the miller's men, remembered the bonus payment he was to get for every man he brought to join the regiment.

"Now how would it be," he cried, waving his tankard in the air, "how would it be if you gave up grinding grain and joined the army? A miller's man is nothing, nobody, lower than dirt—but a soldier, now . . ."

"A soldier," put in the corporal, bringing his fist down on the table so hard that the drummer boy let out a squeak, "a soldier has the time of his life, with regular pay and good company too! And you cut a fine figure in front of the townsfolk, especially the girls and young widows, in your uniform, with shiny buttons on your coat and gaiters above the knee!"

"How about war, though?" asked Tonda.

"War?" cried the lieutenant. "Why, a soldier asks for

nothing better! If his heart's in the right place and he has a bit of luck, he can win both fame and fortune. He'll get a medal, he'll be made corporal or even sergeant for his brave deeds . . ."

"And there's many a man has risen from the ranks in wartime to become an officer, why, even a general!" proclaimed the corporal. "May I be made into mincemeat if I'm not telling you the pure truth!"

"So don't delay!" cried the lieutenant. "Follow us to join the regiment, like the good fellows you are. I'll take you on here and now—done!"

"Done!" The head journeyman shook hands with the lieutenant, and Michal, Merten and all the rest followed suit.

The lieutenant was beaming, while the corporal, none too steady on his feet by now, staggered from man to man feeling their front teeth.

"We have to see if this lot are firm, by thunder! A soldier must have good strong teeth, you know, or he can't bite the ends off his cartridges in battle to shoot the enemies of His Most Serene Highness the Elector, as is his duty to the regiment!"

There was nothing the matter with anyone's front teeth until the corporal came to Andrush, and then he was in some doubt. He gave Andrush's teeth a push and a yank with his thumb, and then it happened.

"By the Grand Turk!" The corporal had pulled two of Andrush's teeth right out. "What's all this, young man? You be a soldier, with a mouthful of teeth like an old woman's? Get away, you and your rotten teeth, or I might forget myself!"

Andrush stayed calm and friendly. "If you don't mind,

those are *my* teeth!" said he. "I'd just like to have them back."

"There you are—you can stick them in your hat!" growled the corporal.

"In my hat?" queried Andrush, in mild surprise. "Dear me, no!" And taking back his teeth, he spat on them and put them back in their proper place.

"They'll be better than ever now. Would you like to convince yourself, sir?"

The miller's men were grinning. The veins on the corporal's temples were swelling with rage, but the lieutenant, thinking of his bonus payment, was unwilling to let Andrush go.

"Go on, take a pull at them!" he encouraged the corporal.

The corporal obeyed orders, although reluctantly, and grabbed hold of Andrush's front teeth. Strange to say, however, hard as he pulled and tugged at them, they wouldn't give the fraction of an inch this time—not even when he tried to knock them out with the stem of his pipe.

"There's something queer going on!" he gasped. "There *must* be something queer going on! Never mind, it's all one to me! It's not for me to decide if this pockmarked fellow is fit to be a soldier, that's your business, sir!"

The lieutenant scratched his ear; he also had had a lot to drink, and Andrush's performance struck him as odd too. "Let's sleep on it," said he. "We'll have another look at this young man before we march away." Then he demanded his bed.

"Very good," said Tonda. "I've made up our Master's own bed for your Worship, and there's a place in the guestroom for his Worship the corporal. But where are we to put their Worships the private soldiers and his Worship the drummer boy?"

"N-never mind that!" said the corporal thickly. "Let 'em sleep in the hay, th-that's good enough for th-them!"

The next morning the lieutenant woke up in a crate of beet root behind the house, while the corporal found himself in the pigs' trough. They both began to curse and swear violently. The miller's men, all twelve of them, came running up, pretending to be perfectly innocent.

Well, well—why, their Worships had been shown to such comfortable beds yesterday evening! Had they been walking in their sleep? It certainly looked like it, what with all the beer they'd had, if one might venture to say so! What luck their Worships hadn't come by any scratches and bruises, if not worse, as they stumbled about the mill! But of course it was well known that a special providence watches over children, fools and drunkards.

"Shut your mouths!" snapped the corporal. "Get out of here—get ready to march away! As for you, you with the pocked face, let's have a feel of those teeth of yours."

Since Andrush's teeth passed the test, the lieutenant had no more scruples about deciding that he was fit for the army, and after breakfast the party of soldiers set off with their new recruits. They marched to Kamenz, where their regiment was stationed, with the lieutenant at the head, followed by the drummer boy, then the miller's men in rank and file, then the two privates, and finally the corporal bringing up the rear. The miller's men were in good spirits, but their companions seemed less cheerful.

The farther they went, the paler their faces grew, and the more frequently did one or the other of them have to disappear into the bushes by the roadside. Krabat, marching at the back with Stashko, heard one of the two privates complain to the other, "By heaven, comrade, I feel as if I'd swallowed ten pounds of glue, there's something lying so heavy on my stomach!"

Krabat exchanged a glance of amusement with Stashko. "That's what comes of swallowing sawdust instead of noodles!" he thought. "And moldy bread instead of meat and crumbs of tobacco instead of herbs and seasoning!"

In the afternoon the lieutenant called another halt at the edge of a little birch wood.

"It's only a quarter of a mile to Kamenz now," said he. "Anyone who wants to disappear, disappear now—it's your last chance. Corporal!"

"Sir?"

"Have the men get their things in order, and keep them from breaking out of rank when we enter the town—and mind they keep in step, in time to the beat of the drum!"

After a short rest, the little troop marched on again, this time to the sound of drum and trumpet . . . trumpet?

Andrush had put his cupped right hand to his lips, puffed out his cheeks, and now he was blowing the Swedish Grenadiers' March. Not the best trumpeter in the world with the finest of all trumpets could have put on a better performance!

His notion caught the fancy of the others, and they too began to play music as loud as they could. Tonda, Stashko and Krabat were performing on the trombone, Michal, Merten and Hanzo played the bugle, and the rest chose trumpets, either large or small, while Juro played the bombardon. Though they were really only blowing through their cupped hands, like Andrush, it sounded as if the entire Royal Swedish Military Band were marching along the road.

The lieutenant tried to shout, "Stop that!" and the corporal opened his mouth to bellow, "Stop it! Stop it this minute, you young scoundrels, you!" But they could not utter a sound, nor could they strike out at the miller's men as they wanted to do. They found they were obliged to stay in their places and march along with the others, the lieutenant at the front, the corporal in the rear, and nothing they could do or say made the least difference.

They entered Kamenz to the sound of bugles and trumpets, much to the amusement of all the soldiers and townsfolk they met in the street. Children came running up and cheered them, the windows of the houses were thrown open, and the girls of Kamenz waved and blew them kisses.

With drums beating, Tonda and his companions, along with their escort, marched several times around the Town Hall Square. It was soon full of onlookers, and finally, alarmed by the sound of the hated Swedish march, Colonel Sir Christian Leberecht Furchtegott von Landtschaden-Pummerstorff, commanding His Most Serene Highness the Elector of Saxony's Dresden Foot, arrived on the scene.

Sir Christian, a veteran grown fat during his years of army service, was followed by three staff officers and several orderlies as he came striding into the market place. He was about to give vent to his indignation in no uncertain terms, on seeing the ridiculous spectacle offered to him, when his breath was taken clean away.

For the moment Andrush spotted the Colonel, he and his companions struck up the March Past of the Swedish Cavalry, which naturally put the old man, as a stalwart commander of infantry in the service of the Elector of Saxony, into a white-hot rage. And since it was a tune that really called for a trot rather than a march, the miller's men and their escort at once started trotting, which looked very funny, except to the Colonel.

Speechless with fury, and gasping for air like a landed fish, Colonel von Landtschaden-Pummerstorff was forced to watch a dozen recruits playing horses in the market place of Kamenz, to the sound of a cavalry march—an enemy cavalry march at that! And what in heaven's name had come over the lieutenant escorting them? He was actually prancing at the rascals' head, with his sword stuck between his knees like a hobbyhorse! In view of such undignified conduct on the part of a Saxon officer, it was hardly surprising to see that his men, drummer boy and corporal included, were not ashamed to join in the capers!

"Squad—halt!" shouted Tonda, when they came to the end of the march. Then the miller's men turned to face the Colonel, waved their caps in the air and grinned at him.

Colonel Sir Christian von Landtschaden-Pummerstorff strode toward them and began to bawl them out like twelve corporals rolled into one.

"You pack of blackguards—who in the devil's name put all this into your heads? The impudence of it! Acting such a farce in public, in broad daylight! Who are you, you young scoundrels? How dare you grin at me! Just let me tell you—me, the Colonel of this great regiment, which has covered itself with glory in thirty-seven battles and a hundred and fifty-nine skirmishes—let me tell you I've a good mind to have these silly capers beaten out of you! I'll hand you over to the military police! I'll have you hauled over the coals! I'll . . ."

"That'll do!" said Tonda, cutting him short. "No need for the military police! Such fine young fellows as my eleven friends here and me aren't cut out for a soldier's life. Fools like him," and he pointed to the lieutenant, "and thick-skinned dolts like that one," (pointing to the corporal), "they may be quite at home in the army, so long as there's no one shooting at them. As for my friends and me, we're made of different stuff! We don't care a bit for you or your regiment, or His Most Serene Highness the Elector either, and you can tell him so if you like!"

Then the miller's men turned into ravens and rose into the air. They circled above the Town Hall Square, croaking, and as a parting gesture they covered Colonel Sir Christian's hat and shoulders—but not with glory.

11 · THE KEEPSAKE

THE SECOND half of October turned warm and sunny again, almost like summer. They used the fine days to bring home several cartloads of peat. Juro put the oxen between the shafts, Stashko and Krabat loaded up the cart with wooden planks and boards, and they took two handcarts along as well. Then Tonda joined them, and off they went.

The peat-cutting was on the far side of the fen, beyond the Black Water. Krabat had been working there with some of the others in the summer, at the hottest time of the year. Since he was inexperienced in the use of the narrow knife they used to cut peat, he had helped Michal and Merten cart the black, greasily gleaming squares of peat out of the hollow and stack them up.

Now the sun was shining, and the birch trees were mirrored in the puddles by the side of their path. The grass on the moorland hills was yellowed, the heather long since faded. A few red berries hung on the bushes, like drops of blood scattered here and there, and occasionally Krabat saw the silver gleam of a late spider's web flung from twig to twig.

Krabat thought back to the old days, to his childhood in Eutrich, and the way they used to gather fallen wood and pine cones on October days like this. Sometimes there were still mushrooms to be found—would he find any today? It was warm enough . . .

When they reached the top of a rise, Juro stopped the oxen. "Here we are. You can unload," he said.

They chose a narrow part of the Black Water, laid boards across and drove them firmly into the bank. Then they laid planks end to end to make themselves a path, and Stashko thrust stout sticks under them to keep them from sagging or giving way at boggy places. But it was further from their footbridge to the peat-cutting than they had estimated, and Juro offered to drive back and fetch the planks they still needed.

"No need for that!" said Stashko. He broke a twig from the nearest birch tree, and then paced out their track, striking the planks with the twig and reciting a magic spell. The planks began to grow longer, until they reached the peat-cutting.

Krabat was fascinated. "Why do we do any work at all?" he cried. "That's what I ask myself, when everything we do with our own hands could be done by magic!"

"Yes, of course," said Tonda. "But think how quickly you'd be bored with a life like that! We can't do without work in the long run, not without going to the dogs."

At the edge of the peat-cutting stood a wooden shack where the dry peat from the year before was stored. The miller's men brought them back to their cart, wheeling them along the planks in the two handcarts, and Juro loaded them up. When the cart was full he climbed up on the box, cried, "Gee up!" and the oxen plodded off at their leisurely pace toward the mill.

While Tonda, Stashko and Krabat waited for Juro to come back, they spent the time bringing the peat cut that summer into the shed and stacking it up. There was no great hurry, and the boy had an idea. He asked the head journeyman and Stashko if they could do without him for a little.

"Where are you going?"

"To look for mushrooms. You only have to whistle and I'll be back at once."

"Well, if you think you'll find any!"

Tonda and Stashko both said he could go. "I hope you have a long knife with you," said Stashko.

"I don't own one, or I'd certainly take it," said Krabat.

"Here, I'll lend you mine," said the head journeyman. "Mind you don't lose it!"

He showed him how to open the clasp knife by pressing a groove on the handle. The blade snapped out; it was dark, almost black, as if Tonda had held it over the wick of a burning candle.

"Your turn." Tonda closed the knife again and handed it to the boy. "Let's see if you have the trick of it."

When Krabat snapped the knife open the blade was spotlessly clean and shining.

"What's the matter?" Stashko asked the boy.

"N-nothing!" he said. But still he was puzzled.

"Off you go, then," Tonda told him, "or those mushrooms of yours will get wind of you and run away!"

They spent four days working at the peat-cutting, and every day Krabat went in search of mushrooms. But all he found were a few very old ones, brown and tough.

"Never mind," said Stashko. "You can't really expect to find mushrooms so late in the year—not unless you give them a helping hand . . ."

He recited a magic spell and turned around seven times, arms outstretched—and immediately about seventy mushrooms sprouted from the peat-cutting, pushing their way up out of the ground like moles, one after another, all in a circle like a fairy ring; beautiful mushrooms of every kind, each as plump and fresh as the next.

"Oh, Stashko!" cried Krabat in amazement. "Do teach me that spell!"

He pulled out Tonda's knife, ready to start picking the mushrooms, but before he could touch them, they shrank, and slipped back into the ground as if someone were pulling them by strings.

"Hey!" cried the boy. "Stop, stop!"

But the mushrooms were gone, and gone for good.

"Never mind," said Stashko again. "Magic mushrooms like that taste bitter as gall, they'd only give you a stomach ache. I nearly did myself in that way last year!"

On the evening of the fourth day Stashko rode back with Juro and the last load of peat, while Tonda and Krabat returned to the mill on foot, choosing a short cut which led them across marshy ground. The first mists were rising from the peat bogs and the pools of water, and the boy was glad when they reached firmer land at last, not far from the Waste Ground.

They could walk side by side now. Usually the miller's men avoided this place, for reasons that Krabat did not know. He remembered his dream of running away. There had been something about Tonda in it, he thought, something about burying the head journeyman, and a place out here.

But that was only a dream. There was Tonda alive and well beside him.

"I want to give you something, Krabat." The head journeyman took his clasp knife out of his pocket. "It's for a keepsake."

"Are you going to leave us, Tonda?"

"Maybe," said Tonda.

"But what about the Master? I don't see him letting you go!"

"There are some things folks don't see happening, yet happen they do!" said Tonda. "There's nothing to be done about it."

"Don't talk like that!" cried Krabat. "Stay here—oh, do stay! I can't imagine what it will be like at the mill without you!"

"And there are things in life folks can't imagine, Krabat," said the head journeyman, "but when they happen we have to manage as best we can."

The Waste Ground was a square clearing, hardly bigger than a threshing floor, with stunted pines growing around it. The boy could make out a row of long, low mounds in the twilight, like graves in some deserted graveyard, untended and overgrown with heather, no cross or stone to mark them—whose graves could they be?

Tonda stopped.

"Take it," he said, handing Krabat the knife, and the boy realized that he could not refuse.

"It has a special virtue," said Tonda. "If you are ever in

danger—real danger—then the blade will not shine when you open it."

"Does it—does it turn black?" asked Krabat.

"Yes," said Tonda, "black—as if you had held it over the wick of a burning candle."

12 · NO PASTOR
OR CROSS

INTER came early after the fine October weather. Two weeks after All Saints' Day it snowed, and the snow settled. Krabat was busy clearing it away again, keeping the path leading to the mill clear. All the same, on the next night of the new moon the Goodman came driving right across the snow-covered meadow in his cart as usual, without getting stuck or leaving any tracks behind him.

The wintry weather did not bother Krabat, for in spite of the snow it was not too bitterly cold, but it seemed to be troubling the rest of the miller's men. Their tempers got worse from week to week, and as the end of the year approached they were more and more difficult to live with. They were touchy and irritable, and would come to blows at the slightest provocation, even the cheerful Andrush, as Krabat learned one day when he knocked Andrush's cap off with a snowball, just for fun—his fingers were itching to do it! Andrush flew at the boy, and would have beaten him black and blue but for Tonda, who stepped in and parted them.

"What impudence!" said Andrush furiously. "No sooner

does he get a bit of down on his chin than he thinks he can be cocky! Just you wait—I'll show you, another time!"

Unlike the others, Tonda was as kind and friendly as ever; the only difference in him that Krabat could see was that he seemed a little sadder than usual, though he tried to hide it from everyone.

"Perhaps he misses the girl he loved," Krabat guessed, and again the singer from Schwarzkollm came unbidden into his mind. It was a long time since he had thought of her. He felt it would be better to forget her altogether, but he did not know how.

The Christmas season came. For the miller's men it was work as usual, and they went about it listlessly and sluggishly. To cheer them up Krabat cut some branches of fir in the wood, to deck the table. When the others came in to eat they were very angry.

"What's this for?" cried Stashko. "Take that rubbish away—get it out of here!"

"Yes, get it out of here!" they all cried. "Take it away!" Even Michal and Merton were shouting.

"Whoever brought this stuff indoors can just get rid of it again!" said Kito.

"And fast!" added Hanzo grimly, "or I'll knock his teeth in!"

Trying to pacify them, Krabat started to explain, but Petar would not let him.

"Just get rid of it, that's all!" he snapped. "Or do we have to take a stick to you?"

Krabat did as he was told, but still it rankled. What in heaven's name had he done wrong? Or was he making too much of a small incident? These days the miller's men were always quarreling, for no good reason, and he must not forget that he was only an apprentice, and an apprentice must expect rough treatment now and then. Only it was odd that he had never been made to feel like that before.

It was only now winter had come that they were all picking on him. Would it be like this for the rest of his apprenticeship—two whole years?

When he had a chance, Krabat asked the head journeyman what was wrong with the others.

"What's the matter with them, Tonda?"

"They're afraid," said Tonda, looking away from him.

"Afraid of what?" Krabat asked.

"I may not talk about it," said the head journeyman. "You'll find out soon enough."

"What about you?" asked Krabat. "*You*'re not afraid, are you, Tonda?"

"More than you guess," said Tonda, shrugging his shoulders.

On New Year's Eve they went to bed earlier than usual. The Master had not put in an appearance all day. Perhaps he had locked himself in the Black Room and was sitting there, as he sometimes did, or he might have gone out in the sleigh. No one seemed to miss him, no one mentioned him.

After supper the miller's men crept away to their straw mattresses without a word. Krabat said, "Good night!" as he did every evening, the way an apprentice should.

Today the others seemed to resent it. "Hold your tongue!" Petar snapped, and Lyshko threw a shoe at him.

"Hey, there!" cried Krabat, sitting up in bed. "Take it easy! Can't I even say good night without . . ."

Another shoe flew through the air, skimming his shoulder. Tonda caught the third.

"Leave the boy alone!" he told them. "This night too will pass." He turned to Krabat. "You'd better lie down and keep quiet, boy."

Krabat obeyed. He let Tonda cover him with the blanket and lay a hand on his forehead.

"Go to sleep now, Krabat—and may all be well with you in the New Year."

Krabat usually slept soundly all night until morning, unless something woke him. This time he woke of his own accord just before midnight. He was surprised to see the lamp burning and the others still awake—all of them, as far as he could see.

They were lying on their beds, and they seemed to be waiting for something. They were scarcely breathing, they scarcely dared to move.

It was deathly quiet in the house—so quiet that Krabat wondered if he had gone deaf. But he was not deaf, for it was then he heard the scream, and the crash down in the hall—and his companions groaned aloud, half in fear, half relieved.

Had there been an accident of some kind? Who had uttered that cry—the cry of a man in deadly danger?

Without stopping to think, Krabat was out of bed, running to fling open the attic door and hurry downstairs to find out.

The door was barred from outside, and however frantically he shook it, it would not open.

Then someone put an arm around his shoulders and

spoke to him. It was Juro, stupid Juro. Krabat knew him by his voice.

"Come, Krabat," said Juro. "Lie down again."

"That scream!" gasped Krabat. "That cry just now!"

"Do you think we didn't hear it too?" replied Juro, leading Krabat back to his bed.

The miller's men were all crouching on their mattresses, staring at Krabat in silence, their eyes wide. No—they were not staring at Krabat, but past him, at the head journeyman's bed.

"Isn't—isn't Tonda here?" Krabat asked.

"No," said Juro. "His place is empty, as you can see. Lie down and try to sleep. And don't cry, do you hear me? Crying won't undo what is done!"

They found Tonda on New Year's Day in the morning. He was lying face downward at the foot of the attic stairs. The miller's men did not seem surprised; Krabat was the only one who could not grasp the fact of Tonda's death. He flung himself on his friend's body, sobbing, calling him by his name and begging, "Say something, Tonda, say something!"

He took the dead man's hand. Only yesterday he had felt it touch his forehead before he went to sleep, and now it was stiff and cold, and strange to him, very strange.

"Get up," said Michal. "We can't leave him lying here."

He and his cousin Merten carried the corpse into the servants' hall and laid it on a plank.

"How did it happen?" asked the boy.

Michal hesitated before answering, "He broke his neck."

"I—I suppose he missed a step—in the dark?"

"Maybe," said Michal.

He closed the dead man's eyes, and put a bundle of straw that Juro had fetched under his head.

Tonda's face was pale. "Like wax," thought Krabat. He could not look at it without feeling tears come to his eyes. Andrush and Stashko took him up to the attic.

"Let's stay here," they suggested. "We'd only be in the way downstairs."

Perching on the side of his bed, Krabat asked what would be done with Tonda now.

"All that ought to be done," said Andrush. "Juro will lay him out—it's not the first time he's done that for someone —and then we'll bury him."

"When?"

"This afternoon, I'd say."

"What, without the Master?"

"We don't need the Master's help to bury him," said Stashko harshly.

That afternoon they carried Tonda out of the mill in a pine coffin, out into the fen of Kosel, to the Waste Ground. The grave was dug already, its sides frosted with rime, the mound of earth beside it dusted with snow.

They buried the dead man hastily and without ceremony, with no pastor or cross, no candles or hymn-singing. The men did not linger by the grave a moment longer than necessary.

Only Krabat stayed on. He wanted to say the Lord's Prayer for his friend Tonda, but somehow it had slipped his memory; he began it again and again, but he could never get to the end of it, not in German nor even in Wendish.

THE
SECOND
YEAR

1·THE CUSTOM
OF THE GUILD

THE MASTER stayed away for the next few days, and during that time the mill stood still. The miller's men lay on their beds or sat by the warm stove. They ate little, and did not say much; they took particular care not to mention Tonda's death, just as if there never had been a head journeyman called Tonda at the mill in the fen of Kosel.

Tonda's clothes lay at the end of his bed, neatly folded and piled up: his breeches, shirt and smock, his belt, his apron and his cap on the top. Juro brought them up on the evening of New Year's Day, and all the men tried to act as if they didn't see the clothes there at all.

Krabat was very downcast; he felt lost and miserable. Tonda's death could not have been an accident, and the longer he thought about it the more certain of that he became. There must be something odd going on here, though he knew nothing about it; something that his companions were keeping from him. What was the secret? Why had Tonda never told him?

Questions kept coming into the boy's mind. If only he

had something to do—idling his time away made him feel quite unwell!

These days Juro was the only busy one among them. He kept the stove alight, did the cooking and saw that meals were served on time, although the others left most of the food on their plates. It must have been the morning of the fourth day when he stopped to speak to Krabat in the hall of the house.

"Like to do something for me, Krabat? You might cut me up some firewood for kindling!"

"All right," said Krabat, following him into the kitchen. There was a faggot of pine wood lying by the hearth, waiting to be cut up small. Juro went to get a knife, but Krabat said he had his own knife with him.

"Even better! Go ahead then—and mind you don't cut yourself!"

Krabat set to work, and it felt as though some strange power were coming from Tonda's knife. Thoughtfully, he weighed it in his hand. For the first time since the New Year he took heart again and felt new confidence welling up within him.

Juro had come up beside him, unnoticed, and was looking over his shoulder.

"That's a good knife you have there," said he.

"It's a keepsake," said the boy.

"A present from a girl, eh?"

"No, from a friend," said Krabat. "I'll never have another friend like him again."

"How can you be so sure?" asked Juro.

"I'm as sure of that as ever I can be of anything," Krabat replied.

The morning after they buried Tonda, the miller's men agreed to make Hanzo head journeyman, and Hanzo gave his consent. The Master stayed away until the eve of Twelfth Night. They were already in bed, and Krabat was about to blow out the light, when the attic door opened and the Master appeared on the threshold, very pale, white as a sheet. He cast a glance around the room, seeming to overlook Tonda's absence—at least, he gave no sign of noticing it.

"To work!" he ordered them. Then he turned around, and was seen no more for the rest of the night.

The miller's men sprang to life, throwing back the covers, jumping out of bed and flinging their clothes on.

"Hurry up, or the Master will be angry!" Hanzo urged them. "You know what he is!"

Petar and Stashko ran to the millpond to open the sluice. The others stumbled down to the grinding room, poured grain into the hopper and set the mill going. As it began to work, with a creaking and a clanking and a hollow thudding, the men felt light at heart.

"The mill is grinding again," thought Krabat, "and life goes on . . ."

They finished work at midnight. When they came back to the attic, they saw someone lying on Tonda's bed: a pale, thin little fellow, with narrow shoulders and a mop of red hair. They surrounded the sleeping lad and woke him, just as Krabat had been woken a year ago. And just like Krabat, a year ago, the red-headed boy was frightened to see eleven ghostly figures standing by his bed.

"Don't be afraid!" said Michal. "We are the miller's men here—you needn't be frightened of us. What's your name?"

"Vitko. What's yours?"

"I'm Michal, and this is Hanzo, the head journeyman. This is my cousin Merten, this is Juro . . ."

When Vitko came down to breakfast next morning he was wearing Tonda's clothes. They fitted as if they had been made for him. He did not seem to be puzzled by that, nor did he ask whose they were before. Krabat thought it was better that way; it made things easier for him to bear.

That evening—the new apprentice had been hard at work in the meal-store all day, and had gone to bed—that evening the Master summoned Krabat and the other men to his room. He sat in his armchair, wearing a black cloak, with two candles burning on the table before him, and a hatchet lying between them. His black three-cornered hat was on the table too.

"I have summoned you here as the rules of the mill and the customs of the guild lay down," said he, when they were all assembled. "If there is an apprentice among you, let him come forward!"

It was a moment before Krabat realized that the Master meant him. When Petar nudged him in the ribs he pulled himself together and stepped forward.

"Your name?"

"My name is Krabat."

"Who will vouch for it?"

"I will," said Hanzo, stepping forward beside Krabat. "I will vouch for this boy and his name."

"One is no better than none!" replied the Master.

Michal spoke up, standing on the other side of Krabat.

"No, but two are a pair, and a pair is surety enough! I will vouch for this boy and his name too."

The dialogue that now went on between the Master and the two journeymen was a series of questions and answers, all in set words. The Master asked the two men whether, where and when the apprentice Krabat had learned the miller's craft, and they assured him that the boy had been properly trained for his trade.

"Do you vouch for that to me?"

"We do," replied Hanzo and Michal.

"Very well! Then we will release this apprentice, Krabat, from his indentures, according to the rules of the mill and the custom of the guild!"

Released from his indentures? Krabat could not believe his ears. Was his apprenticeship really up, after only one year?

Standing up, the Master put on his three-cornered hat. Then he took the hatchet in his hand and went up to the boy. Touching the crown of Krabat's head, and then his shoulders, with the blade of the hatchet, he said solemnly, "In the name of the guild, Krabat, I, your teacher and master, do hereby release you from your former articles of apprenticeship, in the presence of all my journeymen! In future you will be one of them, and will be maintained as a journeyman, according to the customs of the guild."

So saying, he gave Krabat the hatchet; it was the privilege of a free journeyman miller to carry a hatchet at his belt. Then he dismissed them all.

Krabat was surprised and bewildered; all this was completely unexpected. He was the last to leave the room, closing the door behind him. All of a sudden a flour sack was flung over his head, someone seized him by the shoulders and someone else by the legs.

"Off with him to the grinding room!"

That was Andrush's voice. Krabat struggled to free himself—in vain! Laughing and shouting, the others hauled him off to the grinding room and flung him on top of a meal bin. Then they began to work him over. "He's done with his apprenticeship!" cried Andrush. "Now let's put him through the mill, brothers—a journeyman miller must be ground fine!"

They pummeled Krabat like a lump of dough, they rolled him back and forth on the meal bin until he felt quite dizzy, they cuffed and thumped him, and someone hit him quite hard on the head a couple of times, until Hanzo intervened. "That'll do, Lyshko!" said he. "We may put a new journeyman through the mill, but we don't want to kill him!"

When they left off, Krabat felt as if he really had been through a mill. Petar removed the sack, and Stashko scattered a handful of flour on his head.

"Krabat has now duly been through the mill!" Andrush announced. "Thank you, brothers! He's a real journeyman miller now, worthy to be one of us!"

"Good for Krabat!" cried Petar and Stashko, who were the ringleaders along with Andrush. "Up with Krabat!" Once again Krabat was seized by his arms and legs, and the miller's men threw him up in the air and caught him. They tossed him three times, and then sent Juro down to the cellar for wine to celebrate. Krabat had to drink to each of them in turn.

"Here's to you, brother!"

"Your health, brother!"

While the others went on drinking, Krabat sat down on a heap of empty sacks. It was not surprising that his head was throbbing, after all he had been through that evening.

Later, Michal sat down beside him.

"You seem rather puzzled about certain things."

"Yes, I am," said Krabat. "How could the Master release me from my apprenticeship? It *can't* be over already!"

"Ah, your first year in this mill is equal to three in the world outside!" said Michal. "Haven't you noticed how much older you've grown since you first arrived, Krabat? You're exactly three years older now."

"But that's not possible!"

"Yes, it is possible," said Michal, "and other things are possible in this mill too, as you ought to have realized by now."

2 · A MILD WINTER

THE WINTER went on as it had begun, snowy and mild. This year the men did not have much trouble with ice outside the sluice, at the weir and on the millrace; they could break it up quite quickly, and sometimes it would not freeze again for several days. Instead, there were frequent and heavy snowstorms, much to the annoyance of the new apprentice, who could barely keep pace with his job of clearing away the snow.

Looking at young Vitko, who was so skinny and always had a drip on the end of his nose, Krabat realized that Michal must be right when he said he himself had grown three years older, as he really ought to have noticed long before, from the changes in his voice and body, his increased strength and the way hair was sprouting on his cheeks and chin, and had been since the beginning of winter. It looked no more than soft down, but if he stroked it he could feel it distinctly.

During these weeks he kept thinking of Tonda. He missed him all the time, and he was sorry he could not visit his grave. He had tried, twice, and he did not get far either time. There was too much snow out in the fen, and he stuck in it before he could go far. But he was still determined to make a third attempt, the next time he had the chance. Then he had a dream.

It is spring, the snow has melted in the sun and the wind. Krabat is walking through the fen of Kosel. It is night, it is day—the moon is in the sky, the sun is shining. Soon Krabat will reach the Waste Ground. He sees a figure coming toward him through the mist . . . no, it is going away. He believes it is Tonda.

"Tonda!" he cries. "Stop! It's me—Krabat!"

It seems to him that the figure hesitates for a moment. Then, as he walks on, the figure too moves away.

"Tonda, stop!"

Krabat begins to run. He runs as fast as he can go. The space between them narrows.

"Tonda!" he calls.

Now he is only a few paces away—and he finds a ditch at his feet. The ditch is wide and deep, there is no bridge over it, no plank to help him cross.

Tonda is on the other side. He turns his back to Krabat.

"Why are you running away from me, Tonda?"

"I am not running away from you. I am on the other side, as you can see—stay on your side!"

"At least turn your face to me!"

"I cannot look back, Krabat; I am not allowed to. But I can hear you, and I'll answer you. I will answer you three times in all. Now ask me your questions."

What questions? Krabat does not need to think twice.

"Tonda, who brought you to your death?"

"I myself, for the most part."

"And who else?"

"That you will learn, Krabat, if you keep your eyes open. Now for the last question."

Krabat wonders . . . there is so much he would like to know.

"I'm very lonely," he says. "Since you went, I have no friend. Whom can I trust? What do you advise me?"

Even now Tonda does not look at him.

"Go home," says he. "You can trust the very first man who calls you by your name—you may safely rely on him. And one more thing—one last word before I go! It doesn't matter whether you visit my grave or not. I know you are thinking of me, and that is what matters."

Slowly, Tonda raises his hand in farewell. Then he dissolves into the mist and vanishes, without once turning his head.

"Tonda!" Krabat calls after him. "Don't go, Tonda! Don't leave me!"

He shouts as loud as he can—and suddenly he hears someone call, "Krabat! Wake up, Krabat, wake up!"

Michal and Juro were standing by Krabat's bed, bending over him. Krabat did not know if he was awake or still dreaming.

"Who called me?" he asked.

"We did," said Juro. "You should have just heard yourself shouting in your sleep!"

"Did I?" asked Krabat.

"It was heart-rending, it really was!" Michal took his hand. "Do you have a fever?"

"No," said Krabat. "I was just . . . just dreaming. . . . Which of you called my name first?" he added urgently. "Tell me! I must know!"

But Michal and Juro couldn't tell; they said they hadn't noticed.

"Another time we'll count each other out for the privilege of waking you!" said Juro. "Just to make sure there's no doubt about it later!"

Krabat felt sure it must have been Michal who called his name first. Juro was a nice fellow, of course, good-natured through and through, but he was such a fool. Tonda must have meant Michal when he and Krabat talked in Krabat's dream. After this, Krabat turned to Michal when he wanted someone to advise him or answer a question.

Michal did not fail him; he was always willing to tell Krabat what he wanted to know. Only once, when Krabat broached the subject of Tonda, did Michal put him off.

"The dead are dead," said Michal, "and talking won't bring them back to life."

In many ways Michal was like Tonda. Krabat guessed that he was secretly helping the new apprentice, for now and then he would see him standing talking to Vitko, just as Tonda used to stop and talk to Krabat at times last winter, when he helped him by magic.

Juro too took the new apprentice under his wing in his own way, constantly urging him to eat. "Eat up, my boy," he would say, "eat all you can—it'll make you grow tall and strong and put some flesh on those bones of yours!"

The week after Candlemas they went to work in the woods. Six men, Krabat among them, were to bring home the tree trunks they had felled and stacked up last year. This was no easy task in the deep snow. It took them a whole week to clear a way to the place where the trees were stored, even though Michal and Merten, who did valiant work, were in the party.

Andrush could not understand the cousins' enthusiasm. He did only as much work as was necessary to keep him warm.

"If you work so slowly you freeze, you're an ass!" said he. "And if you work so hard you sweat, why, you're worse than an ass, you're a mooncalf!"

It was so warm at noon, those fine February days, that the snow melted enough for the men to get their feet wet out in the woods, and when they came home at night they had to grease their boots well with tallow, working it in with the ball of the thumb, to keep the leather supple; otherwise it would have become rock-hard overnight when the boots hung over the stove to dry.

Each man did this tiresome job for himself, except for Lyshko, who got hold of Vitko and made him do it. When Michal noticed this he took Lyshko to task for it, in front of everyone.

Lyshko merely shrugged it off. "Well, what of it?" he said in an offhand way. "My boots are wet, and what are apprentice boys for if not to work?"

"Not for you!" said Michal.

"Well?" said Lyshko. "It's none of your business to meddle! You're not head journeyman here, are you?"

"No, I'm not," Michal admitted. "But I doubt if Hanzo will mind if I tell you to grease your own boots in the future, Lyshko! Or you might get into trouble—and no one can say I didn't warn you."

Soon after this someone did get into trouble, and it was not Lyshko.

Next Friday evening, when the men were perched in the Black Room in the shape of ravens, the Master said it had come to his ears that one of them was secretly helping the new apprentice, making his work easier, which was forbidden. Such conduct deserved punishment . . . and so saying, he turned to Michal.

"Why are you helping that boy? Answer me!"

"I feel sorry for him, Master. The work you expect him to do is too hard for him."

"So that's what you think, eh?"

"Yes," said Michal.

"You listen to me, then!"

The miller had risen to his feet, and was leaning over the table, resting his hands on the Book of Necromancy.

"What I expect or do not expect of anyone is no concern of yours! Have you forgotten that I am the Master? What I do, I do, and there's an end of it! Now I am going to give you a lesson you will remember all your life! Out, the rest of you!"

He sent the other journeymen out of the room, and shut himself in with Michal.

The others went off to bed, heavy at heart. For half the night they heard dreadful sounds of screeching and cawing echoing through the house. At last Michal came staggering up the attic stairs, pale and haggard.

"What did he do to you?" asked Merten.

Michal made a weary gesture.

"Leave me alone, will you?" he said.

The others had a very good idea who had betrayed Michal to the Master, and next day they held a conference in the meal-store and decided to get even with Lyshko.

"We'll get him out of bed tonight and tan his hide!" said Andrush.

"With a good stout stick apiece!" cried Merten.

"And then we'll shave his head and smear his face with tallow!" growled Hanzo. "And top it all off with soot!"

Michal was sitting in a corner, saying nothing.

"Speak up, do!" cried Stashko. "After all, it was you he told tales of!"

"Very well," said Michal. "I'll tell you what I think."

He waited until they were silent, and then began to speak in a quiet voice, much as Tonda would have spoken in his place.

"Lyshko played me a shabby trick," said he, "but what you're thinking of doing is not much better. Well, no one weighs every word he says in anger! But now it's off your chests, let that be the end of it. I don't want to feel ashamed of the way *you* act!"

3 · LONG LIVE
AUGUSTUS!

HE MILLER'S men did not give Lyshko a thrashing; instead, they left him severely alone. No one spoke to him, no one answered when he asked a question. Juro gave him his oatmeal and his soup in a separate bowl. "You can't expect anyone to share the same dish as a rat!" he said. Krabat agreed; anyone who told tales on his comrades to the Master deserved to be ostracized.

At the next new moon, when the Goodman drove up with his sacks to be ground, the miller had to lend a hand again. He worked very hard, as if to show his men what work really meant—or was it more to impress the Goodman?

The Master was away a good deal in the latter part of the winter, sometimes going on horseback, sometimes taking the sleigh. The men did not know what kind of business he was about, and they did not trouble their heads about it; they had no need to know what didn't concern them, and what they didn't know would do them no harm.

One evening, near St. Joseph's Day, when the snow had melted and it was raining hard, so that the miller's men thought themselves lucky to be sitting in the dry in such vile weather, the Master suddenly ordered his traveling carriage, saying he had to go out on important business, and it was urgent.

Krabat helped Petar put the two bay horses into the shafts, and then held the near horse by the bridle and soothed him. While Petar ran back into the house to tell the Master the carriage was ready, Krabat led the team out to the front yard of the mill. He had flung a horse blanket over his head to keep the rain off, and he put a couple of rugs out for the Master too, in case they were wanted; the carriage was a light one, open at the front.

The Master came striding out, followed by Petar with a storm lantern. He was wearing a voluminous cloak and his black three-cornered hat. Spurs clinked on his boots, and a dagger stuck out under his cloak.

"This is crazy!" thought Krabat, as the Master settled himself on the box. "Does he have to go out in weather like this?"

The Master, who had wrapped himself in the rugs, asked Krabat casually, "Would you like to come?"

"Me?"

"You wanted to know why I was going out, didn't you?"

Krabat's curiosity was stronger than his disinclination to get wet. He was up on the box beside the miller in a twinkling.

"Now, let's see if you can drive!" So saying, the miller handed him the reins and whip. "We must be in Dresden within the hour!"

"Dresden? In an hour?" Krabat could not believe his ears.

"Off we go—drive on!" cried the miller.

They rattled down the bumpy path through the wood. It was pitch dark, like driving through a stove pipe.

"Faster!" the Master urged him. "Can't you drive faster?"

"I'll upset the carriage if I do, Master."

"Nonsense! Hand me the reins!"

And the Master drove on himself . . . how he drove! Out of the wood he went like the wind, and on to the highroad to Kamenz. Clinging to his seat, Krabat had to brace his feet against the footboard. The rain whipped his face, and the wind they made almost swept him out of the carriage.

It had turned misty, and they were racing into the mist; it wrapped itself around them. But before long their heads rose above it, and it sank lower and lower, until it lingered only around the horses' fetlocks.

It had stopped raining, and the moon was shining, but the ground was still veiled in mist, a broad expanse of silvery white, like snow. Were they going across country? Krabat could hear no sound of hooves or clatter of wheels. The jolting and rattling of the carriage had stopped some time ago; he felt as if they were driving over a carpet, or soft snow, or down. The horses stepped out with a smooth, springing stride. It was a joy to drive over the rolling moor in the moonlight like this.

Suddenly there was a jolt that made every joint in the carriage creak. Had they run into a tree stump? A curbstone? What would they do if the shaft was broken, or one of the wheels . . . ?

"I'll just get out and look!"

Krabat already had a foot on the running board when the Master seized hold of him and pulled him back.

"Stay where you are!"

He pointed down. The mists had parted.

Krabat could hardly believe his eyes. Down below him lay the ridge of a roof, and below that a graveyard. Crosses and grave mounds cast their shadows in the moonlight.

"We're stuck on the Kamenz church tower," said the Master. "Mind you don't fall out of the carriage!"

He tugged at the reins and cracked his whip.

"Gee up there!"

Another jolt, and the carriage was afloat in the air again. They went on their way without any more incidents, driving fast and silently through the air, over white clouds gleaming in the moonlight.

"And I took them for mist," thought Krabat.

The clock of the royal chapel was striking half past nine when Krabat and the Master reached Dresden. With a creak, the carriage settled on the paved forecourt of the castle. A groom came running up and took the reins.

"Same as usual, sir?"

"What a stupid question!"

The Master threw the man a coin and then jumped down from the carriage, telling Krabat to follow him into the castle. They hurried up the steps leading to the gate.

At the top an officer barred their way. He was tall as a tree, wearing a broad silk sash, and the moonlight shone on his breastplate.

"Give the password!"

Instead of answering, the Master pushed him aside. The officer put his hand to his dagger to draw it, but he could not; with a snap of his fingers the Master had rooted him to the spot—and there the tall man stood, stiff as a poker, his eyes opened wide, his hand on the hilt of his dagger.

"Come along," said the Master. "That fellow must be new here!"

Inside the gateway, they hurried up a flight of marble stairs, and then through halls and passageways, past walls lined with mirrors and windows with heavy, gold-patterned hangings. The doorkeepers and lackeys they met all seemed to know the Master, for no one barred their way or stopped them to question them. They all stood silently aside, bowed, and let the Master and Krabat pass.

Ever since they had entered the castle Krabat had felt he was dreaming. He was overwhelmed by so much magnificence, by all the brilliance and grandeur around him, and he felt he must look terribly shabby in his miller's smock.

"Are the lackeys all laughing at me?" he wondered. "Are the doorkeepers turning up their noses behind my back?"

He felt something trip him, and he stumbled. What was this? Why, there was a sword between his feet, tripping him . . . whose sword, for goodness' sake? A glance in the nearest mirror stopped him in his tracks. He couldn't understand it. He was wearing a black military tunic with silver buttons, tall leather boots, and—yes, and a sword-belt with a rapier in it! Was that a three-cornered hat on his head? Since when did he wear a white, powdered bag-wig?

He opened his mouth to cry, "Master! What's all this? What does it mean?" But he never uttered the words, for just then they came into a candle-lit anteroom where several gentlemen were standing: army captains and colonels and courtiers with the stars and ribbons of their orders on their breasts.

A chamberlain approached the Master. "Thank heaven you're here at last!" he said. "The Elector is waiting for you! You are not alone?" he added, pointing to Krabat.

"My squire," said the Master. "He can wait here."

The chamberlain beckoned to one of the captains.

"Will you look after the gentleman's squire, sir?"

Taking Krabat's arm, the captain guided him to a small table in one of the alcoves by the windows.

"Will you take wine or chocolate, my dear sir?"

Krabat decided on a glass of red wine, and as the captain and he drank each other's health, the Master entered the Elector's own state apartments.

"Let's hope he succeeds!" said the captain.

"Succeeds in what?" asked Krabat.

"Why, surely you must know—you're his squire! Hasn't your Master been trying to convince the Elector for weeks that His Highness's counselors, who want us to make peace with Sweden, are nothing but fools and he ought to send them packing?"

"Yes, of course," said Krabat hastily, although he had no notion of any of this.

The captains and colonels standing by laughed and drank a toast.

"To the war with Sweden!" they cried. "And may the Elector decide to go on with it! Victory or defeat—but the war with Sweden must go on!"

It was nearly midnight when the Master came back, conducted to the threshold of the anteroom by the Elector himself. "We thank you!" said the Elector. "Your counsel is most valuable to us, as you well know, and though it has taken us some time to open our mind to all your reasons and arguments, the decision is now made. The war goes on!"

The gentlemen in the anteroom rattled their swords and waved their hats in the air.

"Long live Augustus!" they cried. "Glory to His Highness the Elector, and death to the Swedes!"

The Elector of Saxony, a heavy, fleshy man of gigantic build, with the muscles of a blacksmith and fists worthy of any bargeman, thanked his courtiers with a wave of his hand. Then, turning to the Master, he said something to him that no one else caught—what with all the noise in the room, and which probably was not meant for other ears—and with that he dismissed him.

While the courtiers and the army officers stayed behind in the anteroom, Krabat followed the Master out. They left the castle the same way as they had come; past the great windows and the mirror-lined walls, through halls and passageways, down the marble stairs to the gateway, and out onto the steps, where the tall officer still stood, stiff as a poker, eyes opened wide, his hand on the hilt of his dagger.

"Free him, Krabat," said the Master.

Krabat had only to snap his fingers in a way he had learned in the Black School.

"Off with you!" he ordered. "Right about—turn!"

The officer drew his dagger and saluted with the naked blade. Then he turned right, as Krabat had ordered, and marched away.

The carriage was waiting for them on the forecourt of

the castle, and the groom assured the Master that he had carried out his orders and seen to the bay horses.

"So I should hope!" said the Master, and then they climbed up on the box. Only now did Krabat realize he was back in his old clothes again. Well, of course—what would he do with a three-cornered hat, a rapier and a smart military tunic at the mill?

They rattled across the stone bridge over the river Elbe, and once they were out of the city of Dresden and had reached the heights on the other side of the river, the Master drove the carriage off the road. The horses rose from the ground again, and home they drove through the air.

The moon was in the west, very low already, and it would soon go down. Krabat was silent, lost in thought. He looked down at the villages and little towns as they passed over them in their flight, the fields and woods, ponds and streams, the moorland with its bogs and shallow sandy hollow, and all the peaceful countryside lying dark and quiet below them.

"What are you thinking of?" asked the Master.

"I'm thinking of all a man can do with a knowledge of the Black Art," said Krabat. "Why, the Black Art gives you power even over kings and princes!"

4 · AN EASTER CANDLE

ASTER was late that year, falling in the second half of April. The evening before Good Friday Vitko was received into the Black School. Krabat had never seen such a skinny, untidy raven as Vitko made. He thought he could spot a reddish gleam on Vitko's feathers too, but perhaps that was his imagination.

The miller's men spent Saturday sleeping, and late in the afternoon Juro gave them an enormous meal. "Eat as much as you can," Hanzo advised them. "You know it will have to last some time!"

For the first time they let Lyshko share the same dish with them; the rule said that at Eastertide all quarrels among the miller's men must be forgotten.

As dark fell, the Master sent out his men to bring back the sign. Everything happened exactly as it had the year before. Once again the Master counted out his men, once again they left the mill in pairs. This time Krabat's partner was Juro.

"Where do we go?" Juro asked.

"To Baumel's End, if it's all the same to you."

"Very well," said Juro, "so long as you know the way. I'm no use at night—I'd be lucky to find my way from the house to the stable without getting lost!"

"I'll go ahead, then," said Krabat. "Mind you don't lose track of me in the dark."

Krabat had only once before trodden the path they were now taking, and that was with Tonda. It was not difficult to cross the fen, but it might be harder once they came out on the other side of the wood and had to find the path leading over the fields and past Schwarzkollm village. "If worst comes to worst, we'll have to cut across country," thought Krabat. But all went well.

In spite of the darkness they found the path quite easily and went over the fields with the lights of the village to their left. After a while they reached the road on the other side of Schwarzkollm and followed it to the next turning.

"It ought to be somewhere here," said Krabat.

They groped their way along the side of the road, from pine to pine. Krabat was glad when at last his fingers met the squared upright of the wooden cross.

"This way, Juro!"

Juro came stumbling up.

"However did you find it, Krabat? I'd like to see anyone else do that!"

He dug into his pockets, produced flint and steel, and they lit a handful of twigs. By the light of their small fire they gathered pieces of bark and dead branches that were lying under the trees.

"I'll tend the fire," said Juro. "Fires and firewood, now, that's something I *can* deal with."

Krabat wrapped himself in his blanket and sat down under the cross, just as Tonda had sat there a year ago, upright, his knees drawn up, his back against the wood of the cross.

Juro told stories to pass the time, and every now and then Krabat said, "Yes," or "Well, well!" or "Imagine that!" He spoke at random, not really listening, but it was enough to keep Juro happy. Juro talked on, telling stories about anything that happened to occur to him, and it did not seem to bother him that Krabat was hardly attending.

Krabat was thinking of Tonda, and at the same time he was thinking of the girl from Schwarzkollm, the girl who led the choir. She had come into his mind unbidden. He was glad to think that soon he would hear her sing again as her voice floated over from the village at midnight.

But suppose he didn't hear her? Suppose some other girl was singing the solo part this year?

When he tried to remember her voice he made the discovery that he could no longer do so; it was quite vanished from his mind, gone, obliterated. Or did he only think so?

It gave him pain to think he had forgotten her voice, and the pain he felt was of a kind that was new to him—as if he were wounded in a place that he had not known existed until now.

He tried to dismiss it from his mind; he told himself, "I never had much time for girls, and I'm not starting now! What's the good? I'd only go the same way as Tonda some day. There I'd sit, with my heart heavy with grief, and when I looked out at the moonlit moor by night I would sometimes go out of myself in search of the place where my girl lay underground, because I brought her bad luck . . ."

By now Krabat had learned the art of going out of himself. It was one of those few magic arts against which the Master warned his men, "because," said he, "you might easily happen to leave your body and never find your way back." And he impressed it upon his pupils that you could only go out of yourself after nightfall, and you could only return before dawn of the next day.

If you delayed, and stayed away longer, there was no going back. Your body would be closed to you and be buried for dead, while you yourself must wander restlessly between life and death, unable to show yourself, to speak, or make yourself known in any way at all—and that was the peculiar horror of it: even the most insubstantial of poltergeists could at least do some knocking, or rattle pots and pans in the kitchen, or throw logs of wood at the wall.

"No!" thought Krabat. "Whatever may tempt me to go out of myself, I'll take good care not to do it!"

Juro had fallen silent; he was hunched by the fire, scarcely moving. If he had not put a branch on the embers now and then, or fed the fire with a piece of bark, Krabat would have thought he had fallen asleep.

So midnight came.

Once more the Easter bells rang out, far away, and yet again a girl's voice was raised in song in the village of Schwarzkollm—a voice that Krabat knew, the voice he had been waiting for, the voice he had searched his memory for in vain.

Now that he heard it, he wondered how he could ever have forgotten it.

> Christ is risen!
> Christ is risen!
> Hallelujah, hallelujah!

Krabat listened to the girls singing in the village, and to the way the voices chimed in, now the solo voice, then the chorus, and as the chorus sang he was waiting for the solo voice to ring out again.

"I wonder what her hair is like?" he found himself thinking. "Is it brown, or black, or fair as wheat?"

He longed to know; he longed to see the singer's face.

"Suppose I go out of myself?" he thought. "Only for a few moments—just long enough to look into her face . . ."

And already he was reciting the spell, and felt himself shake free of his body as his breath left it. He went out into the black night.

He cast a glance back at the fire, and Juro crouching by it as if he would fall asleep any minute, and himself sitting upright against the cross, neither alive nor dead. All that went to make up Krabat's real life was out here now, outside that body. He felt free, light and untrammeled and alert—all his senses far more alert than ever before.

Still he hesitated to leave his body alone. There was still a last bond to be cut. It was not easy when he knew the separation could be for ever. All the same, he turned away from the young man who bore his name, sitting by the fire, and set out for the village.

No one heard Krabat, no one could see him, but he himself saw and heard everything with astonishing clarity.

Still singing, the girls were walking up and down the village street with lanterns and Easter candles. They wore their communion dresses, all black but for a white headband around the hair, which they wore parted in the middle and combed straight back. Krabat did as he would have done if he had been there in his body; he joined the village lads standing on either side of the street watching the girls, calling out to them and cracking jokes.

"Sing a bit louder, can't you? We can hardly hear you!"

"Watch out for those candles—you'll singe your noses."

"You're blue with cold! Why don't you come over here and get warm?"

The girls acted as though the young men were not there at all. This was their night, and theirs alone. They went calmly on their way, singing, up the street and down again.

Later they went into a farmhouse to warm up. The young men tried to follow them in, but the master of the house turned them away, and they crowded around the window to peer in. The girls were standing by the stove while the farmer's wife gave them Easter cakes and hot milk, and that was all the young men could see, because all of a sudden the farmer was back, with a stout stick this time.

"Shoo!" said he, as if they were stray cats. "Be off with you, my lads, or you'll be sorry for it!"

The young men went away, sulking, and Krabat went too, although he had no need at all to do so. They waited nearby until the girls left the farmhouse and walked on.

By now Krabat knew that the singer had fair hair. She was tall and slender and carried herself proudly, holding her head high. In fact, he could have rejoined Juro by the fire long ago—he *ought* to have rejoined Juro by the fire long ago.

However, he had seen her only from a distance, from the roadside, and now he wanted to look into her eyes. Krabat became one with the flame of the candle that she was carrying. Now he was close to her, closer than he had ever been to any girl before. He was looking into a face that was young and very beautiful in the severe frame of her headband and cap. Her large, soft eyes looked down at him without seeing him—or did they?

He knew it was high time to return to the fire, but the girl's eyes, so bright, fringed by such long lashes, kept him back. He could not tear himself away. He heard her voice only distantly; it did not matter now that he could look into her eyes.

Krabat knew that morning was near, but he could not leave her. He knew his life was lost if he did not break away and return to his body in time—he knew it, but he could not make the effort . . .

Until a sudden sharp pain pierced through him, burning like fire, and wrenched him abruptly away.

Krabat found himself back on the outskirts of the wood, with Juro. A glowing piece of wood lay on the back of his hand, and he shook it off quickly.

"Oh, Krabat!" cried Juro, "I didn't mean to do that! You looked so strange all of a sudden, so different! I lit this torch and shone it in your face. How was I to know that ember would fall on your hand? How bad is it?"

"It'll be all right," said Krabat.

He spat on the burn. He could not tell Juro how thankful he was for his clumsiness. But for that burn he would not be sitting here now! The pain on the back of his hand had made him return to his body as quick as thought, and not a moment too soon.

"Day is breaking," said Krabat. "Let's cut the splinters of wood."

They cut them and put them in the fire.

> I mark you, brother,
> with wood from the cross.
> I mark you
> with the sign of
> the Secret Brotherhood.

On their way back to the mill they met the girls with their pitchers. For a moment Krabat wondered whether to speak to the singer, but then he let it be. Juro was there, and besides, he did not want to frighten her.

5 · THE TALES OF BIG HAT

NCE AGAIN they passed under the yoke at the door, received the blows on their cheeks, and promised to obey the Master in all things. Krabat was not really attending. The singer's eyes haunted him, yet they had looked only at the light of an Easter candle, and never saw Krabat.

"I'll show myself to her another time," he decided. "I want her to know it when she is looking at me."

The last of the men had come back, the water was rushing down into the tailrace, and the mill began to grind. The Master herded his twelve men into the grinding room to set to work.

Krabat did what had to be done, feeling as though it were not really he dragging sacks from the granary, tipping grain into the hopper—a good deal of grain was spilled today—and gradually beginning to sweat. He heard the Master's voice as if through a wall; it did not seem to concern him. A couple of times he collided with one of his companions by mistake, because his thoughts were so far away. Once he slipped on the bottom of the steps leading to the bin floor and hurt his knee; he hardly felt it, but rebalanced the sack that was threatening to slide off his shoulder, and climbed on up.

He was working like a horse; as time went on his feet grew heavy, he felt the sweat dripping from him, he had to strain to lift the heavy sacks, but he did not mind—none of it really seemed to matter. All that was happening at the mill that morning was the business of the old Krabat, the one who had sat all night under the wooden cross; the other Krabat, the one who had been to Schwarzkollm, was indifferent to it. He felt he was a stranger here; none of this had anything to do with him, and he did not understand it.

This time it was Vitko who shouted out in delight first, and gave the signal for general rejoicing.

Surprised, Krabat paused, then spat on his hands and made for the next sack. Juro dug him in the ribs.

"Stop, Krabat!"

Juro's elbow caught him in the exact spot under the left shoulder where it would hurt most. Krabat was breathless for a moment, then he said, "Hey, Juro, you . . . idiot. . . . I'll give you . . . one on the nose for that!" And now it was both Krabats speaking, gasping for breath.

They laughed and drank and ate the rich, golden-brown Easter cakes, and later on they danced.

> Rum-tum-ti-tum,
> The wheel went around,
> And the miller was old,
> And his wits not sound.
> And as it chanced,
> In the month of May,

> He married him a young wife,
> One fine day!
> So around we go,
> As the wheel goes around,
> And the miller was old,
> And his wits not sound!

They danced and sang, and Vitko bawled out the words of the songs as if he meant to outsing every one of them with his shrill, piping voice.

Later, Stashko turned to Andrush and asked him to tell them a story. "One of the tales of Big Hat, maybe?" he suggested.

"Very well," said Andrush. "Just pass the wine!"

He took a long pull at his tankard before beginning his story.

"Well," he began, "one day Big Hat came to the mill at Schleife, and you must know that the miller there was a shocking old skinflint—but now I come to think of it, Vitko may not know who Big Hat is at all . . ."

It turned out that Vitko didn't know, and neither did Krabat.

"Then I must start by telling you about him," said Andrush, and he promised the others to keep it short. "Well," said he, "Big Hat is a journeyman miller, a Wend like us, and I believe he comes from somewhere near Spohla. He is tall, and he is thin, and so old that no one can say for sure just how old he is, but if you were to see him, you'd say he was about forty years old, no more. He wears a gold ring in his left ear, a small, thin ring—you hardly see it unless the sun happens to shine on it. But to make up for that, his hat is enormous, with a broad brim and a pointed crown, and that's how he gets his name. It's by that hat that folks recognize him . . . or else don't recognize him, as you're about to hear. Are you with me?"

Krabat and Vitko nodded.

"You must know, too, that Big Hat is a magician, perhaps the greatest magician there has ever been in Lusatia, and that's saying something. None of us here knows half as much of the Art of Arts as Big Hat has in his little finger. Yet he has remained a journeyman all his life, not wanting to be a master miller or anything greater, like a bailiff or a justice, maybe, or a courtier even, though he easily could have been, if he *had* wanted. But there you are, he didn't. And why not? Because he's his own master, and so he means to remain, a free man going from mill to mill as it suits him in summertime, with no one to give him orders or take orders from him—that's what he likes, and by heaven, that's what I'd like too if I could choose!"

The miller's men all agreed with Andrush. They would all have liked to live like Big Hat, every man his own master, with no need to dance to anyone's tune; they felt that more than ever today, when they had just renewed their promises to the Master, and were bound to the mill in the fen of Kosel for another year.

"Come on, Andrush, your story!" cried Hanzo.

"Right you are, brother—I've been long enough getting started! Just hand me that jug again, and then listen . . ."

"Well," said Andrush, "so Big Hat comes to the mill at Schleife, and he goes up to the miller, who, as I was saying, was the very worst skinflint you ever saw. That man grudged the very butter on the bread and the salt in the soup, and because of that he was always having trouble with his men, since none of them wanted to stay. As everyone knows, you can't work well on poor food for long.

"So along comes Big Hat to this mill, asking for work.

" 'Work enough!' says the miller, and he might have guessed who it was standing there, with the pointed hat and the ring in his ear. But the fact is that those who have to do with Big Hat only remember later what they should have noticed at once. The miller of Schleife didn't notice, for one! So Big Hat hires himself out to this miller for three weeks.

"Well, there were two other men there, and an apprentice boy—thin as sticks, all three of them, with swollen legs from drinking so much water. There was plenty of water to be had at that mill, but that was the only thing the miller didn't begrudge them. They were kept short of bread and even shorter of oatmeal, and there was no meat or bacon at all, only cheese sometimes, and now and then half a herring. The three of them worked like slaves, because they were poor fellows, and the miller had a paper they had signed saying they owed him money, so they couldn't run away.

"Big Hat watched all this for a while. He heard the apprentice crying with hunger every evening until he fell asleep. He saw the two journeymen washing at the pump every morning, and they were so thin that the sun shone through them.

"Then one day, while they were eating their dinner—the mill was running on, for they had just tipped in some buckwheat, which was still being ground—in comes the master just as they're drinking their soup. A thin brew, that soup, with nettles in it, and pigweed, and five or six caraway seeds, maybe even seven! This was Big Hat's moment to tackle the miller.

" 'Hey there, master!' says he, pointing to his soup bowl. 'I've been here two weeks now, and I've had a chance to see what you give folks to eat at your mill. Come, now, don't you think it's rather poor? Try it yourself!' And he offers him his spoon.

"Well, the miller acts as if he can't make out what Big Hat is saying, on account of the noise of the mill; he just points to his ears, shakes his head and grins!

"But the grin was wiped off his face soon enough, for Big Hat knows a trick or two. Big Hat brings the flat of his hand down on the table, and all at once, click! the mill stands still. Quite still, too, with no clattering or rumbling as it runs down. The water is surging through the tailrace, beating against the paddles of the wheel, so it can't be because of someone cranking the sluice down. Some part of the machinery must be stuck, and the miller's praying it isn't the cogwheel or the main shaft. Once he gets over his first fright, the miller is in great alarm. 'Quick!' cries he. 'Quick! Boy, you go and close the sluice—the rest of us will go and see what's wrong with the mill. But hurry, hurry, in heaven's name!'

" 'No need for that,' says Big Hat calmly, and this time he does the grinning.

" 'What?' says the miller. 'Why not?'

" 'Because it was I that stopped the mill.'

" 'Y-you?'

" 'I am Big Hat.'

"As if to order, a sunbeam falls through the window and flashes on a certain gold ring in a certain ear.

" 'You're Big Hat?'

"The miller's knees are knocking. He knows how Big Hat treats master millers who starve and plague their men. 'Good heavens!' he thinks. 'How came I not to notice it when he asked for work? Have I been blind all this time?'

"Big Hat sends him to get paper and ink, and then he writes out what the miller is to give his men from now on.

- Half a pound of bread a day, good weight.
- Every morning, thick gruel made of wheat or millet, buckwheat or barley, cooked in milk, with sugar on Sundays and holidays.
- At dinnertime, plenty of meat and vegetables for everyone twice a week, and on the other days pease pudding, or beans and bacon, or roasted dumplings, or some other nourishing food, whatever is to be had, and plenty of it, with all the proper seasoning. . . .

"He wrote and wrote, and it was a long list, laying down exactly what the miller of Schleife was to give his men in the future. 'Put your name to that,' said Big Hat, when the list was done, 'and swear to do as it says!'

"So, knowing he had no choice, the miller put his name to the paper and swore.

"Then Big Hat took the spell off the mill. Bang! went his hand on the table, and the mill was working again. He gave the list to one of the journeymen to keep, and he said to the miller—this time the miller could hear him quite clearly, in spite of the noise of the mill—'Let's be sure we understand each other, master! You've sworn a solemn oath; mind you don't break that oath when I leave, or else—' and click! the mill stood still again, with not a rattle or a clatter as it ran down, so that the miller was petrified with fright. 'But,' said Big Hat, 'the mill will stand still forever then—no one will ever be able to get it going again! Just remember that!' So saying, he set the mill working once more and went his way.

"Ever since then, folks say, the men who work at the mill in Schleife have lived off the fat of the land. They get properly fed, none of them goes hungry, and their legs are no longer swollen with water."

The miller's men all liked Andrush's story. "Go on!" they demanded. "Tell us more! Have another drink, and then let's hear some more about Big Hat!"

Andrush raised his tankard to his lips, to moisten his throat, and then he went on telling tales of Big Hat, and how he paid out the master millers in Bautzen and Sohrau, in Rumburg and Schluckenau, all for fun and to do the miller's men good.

Krabat found himself thinking of their own master and his journey to Dresden to visit the Elector, and he wondered how it would be if Big Hat ever came to visit the master of the mill in the fen. If it came to a trial of strength between them, which of the two would win?

6 · HORSE TRADING

AFTER EASTER they began to overhaul all the woodwork of the mill. The Master put Stashko in charge, since he was the most skillful carpenter among them, with Kito and Krabat as his assistants. They inspected everything that was made of wood, from the meal-store to the roof, and where they found anything in need of repair—a post that was about to break, a loose board, woodworm in the flooring—the three of them replaced it or repaired the damage. There was a lot of work to be done on the woodwork down by the millrace; the weir needed rebuilding, and they were to make a completely new water wheel too.

Stashko and his assistants did nearly all the work with their hatchets, as self-respecting journeyman millers would always do, reaching for a saw only when it was absolutely necessary, and then reluctantly.

Krabat was glad he had work that hardly allowed him time to think of "anything else"—that is to say, the singer of Schwarzkollm. All the same, he found himself thinking of her quite often, and sometimes he was afraid the others would notice. Lyshko was already suspicious, for one. One day he asked Krabat what was the matter with him.

"The matter?" asked Krabat. "What do you mean?"

"Well, these days you hardly listen when anyone speaks

to you. I once knew a man who was in trouble over a girl; he was the same way!"

"And *I* once knew a man who could hear the grass growing!" said Krabat, as casually as he could. "Or so he said—but it was just the straw crackling inside his head!"

Krabat was working hard in the Black School, and soon he knew as much of the Secret Arts as most of his fellow journeymen. Only Hanzo, Merten and Michal were still ahead of him, especially Michal, who had been a star pupil ever since the New Year, and had far outstripped all the others.

The miller was obviously pleased with Krabat's industry; he often praised him, and encouraged him to keep it up. "I can tell that you'll go far," he said one Friday evening in May, after the lesson. "In my opinion, you have more aptitude for the Secret Arts than most, or I'd never have taken you to the Elector's court with me!"

Krabat was proud of the Master's praise; he was only sorry he didn't have more chance to make use of the knowledge of magic he had gained.

"Well, we can put that right!" said the Master, as if he could hear Krabat's thoughts. "Tomorrow you will go to Wittichenau market with Juro and sell him as a black stallion for fifty guilders. But mind that fool Juro doesn't give you any trouble!"

Next day Krabat and Juro set off for Wittichenau. Krabat was thinking of Master Blaschke from Kamenz, and whistling to himself. Horse dealing promised to be good fun. He thought it strange when he realized Juro was getting steadily unhappier as they went along.

"What's the matter?" he asked.

"What do you mean?"

"You look as if you were going to the gallows!"

"What's to become of me?" asked Juro, blowing his nose. "I'll never do it, Krabat—I never turned myself into a horse before."

"It can't be all that difficult, Juro," said Krabat. "I'll help you."

"But what good will that do?" Juro had stopped and was looking at him sadly. "All right, so we turn me into a horse, you sell me for fifty guilders, and that's that—for you, Krabat, but not for me! And why not? Simple! How do I change back from being a horse without your help? It's almost as if the Master puts me into this fix to get rid of me!"

"Good gracious, what nonsense you do talk!" said Krabat.

"No, I don't!" said Juro. "I'll never do it, I'm far too stupid!"

He looked the picture of misery, standing there hanging his head.

"Well, suppose we change places?" suggested Krabat. "So long as the Master gets his money, that's the main thing; he can't mind which of us sells which!"

Juro was delighted.

"Would you really do a thing like that for me, Krabat?"

"Never mind that!" said Krabat. "Just promise not to tell anyone, and the rest of it should be easy."

They went on their way, whistling, until they saw the roofs of Wittichenau ahead. Then they turned off the road, and went behind a barn. "This is a good spot," said Krabat. "No one will see us here when I turn myself into a black horse. Now, you know that you mustn't sell me for less than fifty guilders, not on any account. And before you let me go, take the halter off me, or I'll have to stay a horse all my life, and I don't fancy the idea of that!"

"Never fear!" said Juro. "I'll remember. Stupid I may be, but not that stupid!"

"Good," said Krabat. "Don't forget, then."

Muttering a magic spell, he changed himself into a black horse with a magnificent saddle and bridle.

"Just look at you!" cried Juro. "You should be on parade!"

The horse dealers in Wittichenau market opened their eyes and mouths wide and came running up when they saw the black stallion.

"How much?" they asked.

"Fifty guilders."

Before long a dealer from Bautzen was willing to pay the asking price. Then, just as Juro was about to cry, "Done!" a stranger joined in the bargaining. He was a gentleman who looked like a man of rank, or a retired army officer, wearing a Polish cap and a red riding coat with silver lacing.

"You're going to make a bad bargain there!" said he to Juro in a hoarse voice. "Why, your stallion's worth far more than fifty guilders! I'd give you a hundred!"

The dealer from Bautzen was furious. Why did this crack-brained fellow have to cross his path? Who was he, anyway? No one knew the stranger who looked like a nobleman, but was not—no one but Krabat.

Krabat had recognized him at once, by the patch over his left eye and by his voice. He blew out his nostrils and pranced back and forth. If only he could warn Juro! But

Juro did not seem to notice Krabat's uneasiness; he was thinking of the hundred guilders.

"Why do you hesitate?" the stranger pressed him. And bringing out a purse, he tossed it to the young man. Juro bowed.

"Thank you kindly, sir!"

Next moment the stranger made a grab for the halter, tore it out of the bewildered Juro's hands, and with one leap he was up on Krabat's back, digging the spurs into his flanks so hard that the horse reared, whinnying.

"Stop, sir, stop!" cried Juro. "The halter! You have to leave me the halter!"

"Certainly not!" The stranger burst out laughing, and then even Juro recognized him.

Bringing his riding whip down hard on Krabat, the Master cried, "Gee up, there!" And taking no more notice of Juro, he shot away.

Poor Krabat! The Master rode him hard all over the moor, over stock and stone, over hedges and ditches, through thorns and mire.

"I'll teach you to disobey me!" he cried.

When Krabat flagged, the miller cut him with the whip, driving the spurs in so deep that the young man felt as if red-hot nails were being driven into his flesh.

Krabat tried to shake the Master off, he bucked, he tore at the bridle, he stopped dead.

"Try it, go ahead, try it!" shouted the Master. "You won't throw me!"

Using his whip and spurs, he wore Krabat out. One last attempt to throw off his rider failed, and Krabat gave up the fight. His mane was dark with sweat, and there was foam at his mouth; his whole body was steaming and he was trembling and wheezing. Blood flowed from his flanks; he could feel the warmth of it running down the inside of his thighs.

"That's better!" said the Master.

He collected Krabat and then made him trot. A gallop to the right, a gallop to the left, back again at a gentle trot, a short way at a walking pace, and then they stopped.

"You might have made that easier for yourself." The miller dismounted and untied the halter. "Now turn yourself back into a man!"

Krabat changed back, but he was still covered with welts, cuts, wounds and bruises.

"That's the punishment for your disobedience! When I send you on an errand you're to carry it out, exactly as I told you and no other way. You won't get off so lightly another time! Remember that!"

There could be no doubt that the Master meant what he said.

"And one thing more!" He raised his voice a little. "No one's stopping you from getting your own back on Juro— there you are!"

He pressed his riding crop into the young man's hand. Then he turned to go, and after taking a few steps he rose into the air as a hawk, and soared swiftly away.

Krabat limped homeward. He had to stop after every few steps he took. Leaden weights seemed to hang on his feet, every bone in his body hurt, every muscle was painful. When he reached the Wittichenau road he let himself drop in the shadow of the nearest tree and rested. What would the girl from Schwarzkollm say if she could see him now?

After a while Juro came jogging along the road, very subdued, looking guilty.

"Hey there, Juro!" Krabat called. The poor fellow was alarmed.

"Is that really you, then?"

"Yes," said Krabat, "it's really me."

Juro retreated a step, pointing to the riding crop with one hand and shielding his face with the other.

"I suppose you're going to thrash me?"

"I ought to!" said Krabat. "That's what the Master expects me to do, anyway."

"Hurry up, then!" said Juro. "I've deserved my beating—I'd like to get it over with!"

Krabat pushed the hair back from his forehead. "Would it make my own skin heal any faster, do you think?"

"What about the Master, though?"

"He didn't *order* me to thrash you," said Krabat. "It was just a suggestion. Come here and sit down beside me, Juro."

"Very well," said Juro.

He took something that looked like a piece of wood out of his pocket, and with it he drew a circle around the place where they were sitting. Then he drew three crosses and a pentagram within the circle.

"What are you doing?" asked Krabat.

"Oh, nothing!" said Juro evasively. "It's just to protect us against gnats and midges. I don't like to be bothered with them. Let's have a look at your back!" So saying, he lifted Krabat's shirt. "Dear me, the Master gave you a bad time and no mistake!"

Whistling through his teeth, he searched his pockets.

"I ought to have some ointment here, I always carry it with me. It's a recipe of my grandmother's . . . would you like me to put some on your back?"

"If it'll do any good," said Krabat.

"At least it can't do any harm," Juro assured him. Carefully, he rubbed the ointment into Krabat's wounds. It was pleasantly cool, and made the pain fade quickly. Krabat felt as if he were growing a new skin.

"What wonderful ointment!" he cried in surprise.

"Ah, well, my granny," said Juro, "my granny, now she was a clever woman. We're a very clever family, Krabat, all but me. When I think that you might have had to stay a horse all your life because of my folly . . ." He shuddered and closed his eyes.

"Stop that!" Krabat told him. "We were lucky, after all!"

They went peaceably home together, and when they were almost through the fen, just before they reached the mill, Juro began to limp.

"You'd better limp too, Krabat."

"Why?"

"We don't want the Master to know about that ointment. We don't want anyone else at all to know."

"What about you?" asked Krabat. "Why are *you* limping?"

"Because you gave me a thrashing, and don't you forget it!"

7 · WINE AND WATER

THEY BEGAN to build the water wheel at the end of June. Krabat helped Stashko measure the old mill wheel, since the new one must be exactly the same in all its parts; when it was finished they were going to fit it on the existing axletree. Their carpenter's shop was behind the stable, between the barn and the shed, and they spent all their time there now, making the wheel—the spokes and the felloes forming the outer rim, the paddles and the pegs that held them in place. Stashko showed them how to do it.

"Everything must be just right," he told his assistants, "or we'll be a laughingstock the day we set the new wheel in place!"

It was light until late in the evening now, and in fine weather the miller's men would often sit out of doors, outside the mill, while Andrush played his jew's-harp.

These days Krabat felt he would like to go to Schwarz-kollm again. Maybe the singer would be sitting outside her house, maybe she would wave in reply to his greeting as he went by. Or perhaps she was with the other village girls, and they were singing again. Many evenings, when the wind was blowing from Schwarzkollm, he thought he could hear singing in the distance, but that couldn't really be possible, not with the wood in between.

If he could only find some excuse to get away, a good, innocent reason that would not arouse even Lyshko's suspicions! It was possible that such a reason might present itself some day, and then he would not be making anyone suspicious, and so placing the girl in danger.

When all was said and done, he knew very little about her. He knew what she looked like now, the way she walked and held her head, and the sound of her voice—he knew all this as well as if he had always known it. He knew too that he could never put her out of his mind and out of his life again, no more than he could banish the memory of Tonda.

Yet he did not even know her name.

Now and then he wondered what it was, and it gave him pleasure to think of a name for her. Milenka . . . Radushka . . . Dushenka was a good name; it would suit her.

"And it's as well I don't know her real name," thought Krabat. "For if I don't know it I can't give it away, not awake nor in my sleep, as Tonda made me promise—it seems a thousand years ago that we sat by the fire that Easter night, he and I."

Krabat still had not visited Tonda's grave. One summer's day he woke at the first light of dawn, stole out of the mill and went out into the fen. There were dewdrops hanging on every blade of grass and every twig, and wherever Krabat passed he left a dark trail in the grass behind him.

At sunrise he came to the edge of the Waste Ground, not far from the spot where he and Tonda first reached firm land when they were coming back from the peat-cutting. On the way Krabat had picked a few ragged robin flowers from the bank of a pool in the swamp, to put on Tonda's grave. But when he saw the row of long, low mounds ahead of him in the morning sunlight, they were all alike; there was no way to tell them apart. Was Tonda buried to the left of the row, or the right? And the mounds were not evenly spaced, so it could be that Tonda's grave lay somewhere in the middle.

Krabat was at a loss. He could not remember anything that might give him a clue. The day they buried Tonda everything around them had been white, covered with snow.

"That's that, then," he thought.

He walked slowly past the mounds, laying a flower on each one. At the end there was one flower left over. He twisted its stem in his fingers and said, looking down at it, "For the next man we bury here . . ."

He let the flower fall—and it was only then, in the brief time it took to reach the ground, that he realized what he had just said. He felt a thrill of horror, but there was no unsaying it now, and the flower lay where it fell, at the far end of the row, between the mound on the extreme right and the wood.

Back in the mill no one seemed to know where Krabat had been, yet someone had been watching him secretly after all: Michal. That evening he spoke to Krabat in private.

"The dead are dead," said Michal. "I told you so once

before, and tell you so again. Those who die at the mill in the fen of Kosel are forgotten as if they had never been—that's the only way the others can go on living, and life must go on. Promise me to remember that!"

"I promise," said Krabat, and he nodded. But even as he nodded he knew he neither could nor would keep that promise.

Work on the new water wheel took a full three weeks in all. They did not use a single nail; the parts were all made to fit exactly, and mortised together. Later, when they brought the wheel to the water, the tenons would swell and hold better than any glue.

For the last time Stashko checked that the measurements were all exact, and nothing left undone. Then he went to tell the Master that the wheel was ready.

The Master fixed the next Wednesday as the day to set the wheel in place. By rights he ought now to have sent word to all the other millers in those parts, inviting them and their journeymen to his mill on the great day—that was the custom. But the master of the mill in the fen did not hold with such customs, and he did not care a hang for the other local millers. "What do we want with strange folks at our mill?" said he. "We can set the wheel in place well enough by ourselves!"

Stashko, Krabat and Kito had plenty to do before Wednesday. The old water wheel and the tailrace had to be covered with good, strong scaffolding, they had to see that the ropes, winch and pulley were in order, and to provide poles on which to carry the wheel, levers and so forth.

On Tuesday evening the miller's men wove leaves through the spokes of the new wheel, and Stashko added a few flowers as a finishing touch. He was proud of his work, and didn't mind showing it.

Wednesday began with bacon cakes for breakfast. "Thinks I to myself, you'll get down to work better with something good inside you!" said Juro as he served them out. "So eat your fill—but don't overeat, now!"

After breakfast they went off to their carpenter's shop, where they found the Master waiting for them. They passed poles through the wheel, as Stashko had shown them, three on one side of the hub and three on the other.

"Ready?" called Stashko.

"Ready!" cried the miller and his men.

"Good luck, then—off we go. Lift away!"

So they carried the wheel off to the millrace and put it down on the grass beside the scaffolding. "Gently, now!" said Stashko. "Take it easy; mind it doesn't slip out of joint."

Michal and Merten clambered up on the scaffolding, and with the help of the pulley and several ropes they shifted the axletree and secured it to the crossbeam behind the old wheel. Now, using poles and levers, the men lifted the mill wheel off the axle and out of the tailrace, and carried it away.

The new water wheel was set upright, brought over to the tailrace and lowered into it, until the hub was level with the axletree. They now had to fit the hub of the wheel onto the axle. Stashko was sweating with excitement. He had climbed right down into the tailrace, along with Andrush, and was issuing orders from there. "Over to the left a bit . . . take it slowly . . . now a little lower, to the right . . . mind you don't topple it over!"

Up until now all had gone well—but suddenly Andrush

struck his hands together and uttered an oath. "Just look at that!" he called to Stashko. "See what a mess you made of it!" And he pointed to the hole in the middle of the hub. "You might get a broomstick through it, maybe, but the axle will never fit in!"

Stashko, horrified, went red as fire. He had measured everything so carefully and precisely, and in spite of that the hole in the hub was far too small, so small that even Juro couldn't help but see it!

"It . . . I . . . I can't understand it!" stammered Stashko.

"Can't you?" asked Andrush.

"Not for the life of me!" said Stashko.

"Well, I can!" said Andrush, grinning.

By now the others had all realized he was just playing a trick on Stashko. He snapped his fingers, and at once everything was all right again—the hole in the hub was the right size, and when they placed the wheel on the axle it fitted like a glove.

Stashko bore Andrush no ill will for his trick; he was glad the most difficult part of the job was over. By comparison, the rest was child's play. They restored the axle to its usual position and took the ropes away. Then the wheel was driven firmly onto the axletree and the wedges knocked in. A few blows with a mallet, and it was done.

The miller had been lending a hand, like all the others. Now he climbed up on the scaffolding and told Juro to bring him some wine. Standing above the tailrace, the Master raised his tankard, drank to his men, and poured the rest of his wine over the garlanded wheel.

"First wine, then water!" he cried. "Start it going!"

Hanzo opened the sluice, and to the acclamation of the miller's men, the new wheel began to go around.

After their work, the men carried the long table and the benches from the servants' hall out to the yard in front of the mill, and Lyshko helped Vitko bring out the Master's armchair, which they set at the head of the table. Then they washed in the millpond, and while the other men cleaned up and put on fresh shirts and smocks, Juro was making the final preparations for a festive meal.

There was roast meat and wine, to celebrate the setting of the new wheel in place. They sat out in the open until late in the evening. The Master was in a good mood, and feeling talkative. He praised Stashko and his assistants for their work, and even had a good word for stupid Juro—he told him the roast was excellent and the wine did him good. He sang and cracked jokes with his men, urged them to drink, and he himself drank most of all.

"Be merry!" he shouted. "Be merry, my lads! Anyone who saw you might well be envious! You don't know your luck!"

"What, us?" cried Andrush, clapping a hand to his head. "Listen to that, friends, the Master envies us!"

"I envy you your youth." All of a sudden the Master was serious, but not for long. He began to tell them a story of the days when he himself was a journeyman miller, and about Krabat's age.

"I had a good friend in those days, called Jirko. We learned our trade together at the mill in Commerau, and then we went on our travels together, all over Lusatia, into Schleswig, as far as Bohemia. When we came to a miller's place we always asked if he had work for two of us; it would never have done for us to be separated, Jirko and I. It was better to stick together, and merrier too. Jirko always saw that we had something to laugh at. And

how he could work! He could work for three if he had to!
As for the way the girls ran after us, you'd never believe
it!"

The Master was in full swing. Now and then he paused
to drink, and then picked up the thread of his story again
and went on. He told how one day he and Jirko came to a
Black School, how they spent seven years learning the
magic arts, and when that time was over, they began to
travel around the country once again.

"And so," said the Master, "we took service at a mill
near Coswig, and the Elector came riding by with a hunting party one day and stopped to rest in the meadow
behind the millpond, in the shade of the trees.

. "We journeymen, Jirko and myself included, stood behind the bushes watching them eat. Two servants had
spread a tablecloth on the grass, and the Elector and his
guests sat around it and ate from silver plates, which the
servants put before them. There were quail pasties with
truffles, and game, and three sorts of wine to drink, and
after that there were sweetmeats, and they had brought it
all with them in enormous baskets, loaded on pack horses.

"Well, when the Elector—he was a young man himself
at the time—when he and the ladies and gentlemen had
had enough to eat, he gave a loud belch, just to show he'd
eaten well. Then he said this meal out of doors had done
him so much good, he felt as strong as twelve oxen. And
seeing us young fellows standing gaping in the bushes, he
shouted out to us for someone to bring him a horseshoe,
and quickly, or he'd burst with his own strength!

"We knew that the Elector was said to be able to break
a horseshoe with his bare hands—crack! right down the
middle. So we could guess why he wanted one, and Jirko

ran to the mill and fetched him a horseshoe from the stable.

" 'Here you are, Your Most Serene Highness!'

"The Elector grasped the horseshoe by both ends. The huntsmen, who were sitting a little way off with the horses and hounds, had already jumped up, pursed their lips and raised their horns, and at the moment when the Elector broke the horseshoe, they began to blow with all their might, puffing out their cheeks like bellows. To the sound of the hunting horns, the Elector held up the two halves of the horseshoe and showed them to the company. Then he asked the gentlemen in his hunting party if any of them could do it.

"Well, they all said no to that, but Jirko was feeling his oats. He went right up to the Elector and claimed, 'By your leave, I can do better than that! I can put the horseshoe together again.'

" 'Any blacksmith can do as much!' says the Elector.

" 'With a pair of bellows and a fire in his forge, yes!' Jirko grants him. 'Not with his bare hands!'

"Without waiting for the Elector's reply, he just took the two halves of the horseshoe away from him. Then, pressing the broken surfaces together, he spoke a charm.

" 'There, if it please you!' said he.

"The Elector snatched the shoe out of his hand and examined it. It was whole again, all of a piece.

" 'Humph!' growled the Elector. 'You can't fool us into thinking that will hold!'

"He tried to break the horseshoe for the second time, thinking it couldn't be hard to do. But he was reckoning without Jirko! He tugged and tugged at that shoe until the veins of his throat stood out like ropes. Sweat was dripping from his brow, and his eyes were bulging out of his head. First he went red in the face as a turkey cock, then purple, and finally dark blue. His lips were white with the strain, thin and white as two chalk lines.

"Then, suddenly, his Highness the Elector dropped the horseshoe—and was yellow as a quince with anger.

" 'To horse!' he ordered. 'We'll ride on!'

"His Most Serene Highness was so unsteady on his feet, he could hardly get into the saddle. And ever after that he gave the mill near Coswig a very wide berth indeed!"

The Master went on drinking and telling tales, tales of his life when he was a young man, and tales of Jirko, until Michal asked him what had become of this Jirko. By then it was late, the stars were in the sky and the moon was rising behind the stable roof.

"What became of Jirko?" The Master clasped his tankard in both hands. "I brought him to his death."

That made the young men sit up.

"Yes, I brought him to his death," repeated the Master, "and one of these days I'll tell you how it happened. But now I'm thirsty—wine, more wine!"

The Master drank steadily on, without another word, until he fell back in his chair, rigid as a corpse.

The sight of him filled the men with dread. They could not bring themselves to carry him into the house; they left him sitting there until he woke of his own accord next morning and crawled off to bed.

8 · THE COCKFIGHT

OW AND THEN traveling journeymen
would come to the mill in the fen and ask the
miller for food and lodging; that was the custom, and it was their right to ask it—not that
they had much luck with the Master. Though
he was in duty bound to give the travelers food for a day
and shelter for the night, he did not observe the customs of
his guild. Instead he showed them the door, with harsh
words.

"I want nothing to do with a pack of waifs and strays,"
he snapped at them. "I have neither bread nor gruel for
the likes of you, and you'd better get out at once, or I'll set
the dogs on you and hunt you all the way to Schwarzkollm!"

This was generally enough to get rid of the unwanted
guests, but if one of them turned awkward, the miller
knew how to make the poor fellow believe he was being
chased by dogs, whereupon he would strike out frantically with his staff and make off, yelling.

"We don't need snoopers here," the Master used to say.
"We can do without useless mouths to feed too!"

It was a heavy, sultry day in high summer. A haze hung
over the fen, and the air was so close that it was difficult

to breathe. A strong smell of weeds and stagnant water rose from the millrace; soon a storm would break.

Krabat had settled down after dinner in the shade of the willows on the bank of the millpond. He was lying on his back in the grass chewing a stalk, with his hands clasped behind his neck. He felt tired and sleepy, and his eyes closed.

Just as he was dozing off, he heard someone come up the path whistling loudly. When he opened his eyes he saw a traveling journeyman before him.

The stranger was a tall, thin man, rather middle-aged, with skin as dark as a gypsy's. He was wearing an odd sort of tall, pointed hat, and a narrow gold ring in his left ear, but otherwise he looked like any other journeyman miller on his travels, with wide linen trousers, a hatchet in his belt, and his bundle on a strap over his left shoulder.

"Good day, brother!" said he.

"Good day," said Krabat, yawning. "Where are you from, and where are you going?"

"I've come from there, and I'm going thither!" said the stranger. "Take me to your master!"

"You'll find him in his room," replied Krabat lazily. "First door on the left when you get into the hall. You can't miss it."

The stranger regarded Krabat with a mocking smile.

"Just do as I ask, brother! Take me to him."

Krabat felt an irresistible power issuing from the stranger; it forced him to get up and show the man the way, as he was asked.

The miller was sitting in his room, at the head of the table, and he looked up in annoyance when Krabat brought the stranger in, but the man did not seem at all disturbed.

"By your leave!" said he, raising his hat. "Good day to you, Master, and according to the custom of the guild I ask for lodging for the night, and food for my journey."

The Master showed him the door in his usual way, but the stranger took no notice.

"Never mind all that about the dogs!" said he. "*I* know you don't have any! May I sit down?"

And without more ado he sat down on the chair at the foot of the table. Krabat simply could not understand it. Why was the Master putting up with such treatment? Normally he'd be up on his feet, chasing the stranger away from the mill with a stick if need be—why not this time?

The two men sat there in silence, staring at one another across the table. They looked dangerous, as if they would be at each other's throats any moment, knives drawn.

Outside there was the first growl of thunder, still far away; a muffled growl, only just audible.

Then Hanzo came through the door, followed by Michal and Merten. One by one the miller's men came into the room, until they were all present. Later they told each other that they suddenly wanted to see the Master—quite by chance the same idea had occurred to every one of them, and brought them in.

The storm was coming closer; a gust of wind rattled the window frames, and there was a flash of lightning. Pursing his lips, the stranger spat on the table—and where he spat, there was a red mouse sitting.

"Now, miller, beat that if you can!"

The Master spat, and there was a black mouse on the table, one-eyed like the miller himself. The mice circled one another on nimble paws, trying to bite each other's tails. Just as the black mouse was about to sink its teeth in, the stranger snapped his fingers.

Where the red mouse had been, there was now a red tomcat, crouched ready to spring. In an instant the black mouse turned into a tomcat too, black and one-eyed. Spitting, with their claws out, the two went for each other, clawing, biting and clawing again.

The red cat was aiming for the black cat's eye. Yowling, he pounced upon his enemy, and almost scratched it out.

This time it was the Master who snapped his fingers, and instead of the black cat there was a black rooster on the table. Beating its wings, slashing with beak and claws, it attacked the red cat, making it flinch back—but not far, for now the stranger snapped his fingers again.

There were two roosters facing one another on the table, a black one and a red one, combs swollen, feathers ruffled.

Outside the storm broke, but the miller's men took no notice of it. A furious fight broke out between the two roosters. Fluttering wildly, they flung themselves into the fray. There was a flurry of thrusts with beak and spurs, they flapped their wings, making the feathers fly, and screeched and crowed.

Finally the red rooster managed to get on the black one's back. He dug his spurs into his enemy's feathers, tearing at him unmercifully, striking out furiously with his beak, until the black rooster turned to escape. The red rooster chased him through half the mill and out into the fen.

There was one last tremendous flash of lightning, and a roll of thunder like a thousand drums; then there came a sudden lull, with no sound but the rain beating down outside the windows.

"You've lost, miller!" said the stranger. "Now then, I'm hungry—bring me something to eat, and don't forget the wine!"

White as a sheet, the Master rose from his chair. With his own hands he brought the stranger bread and ham, smoked meat and cheese, pickled cucumber and onions. Then he fetched a pitcher of red wine from the cellar.

"Too sharp," said the stranger, tasting it. "Bring me some wine from the little cask in the right-hand corner at the back, the one you've been keeping for special occasions! This is a special occasion!"

Grinding his teeth, the miller obeyed orders; he had lost the contest, and must submit.

The stranger enjoyed his meal while the Master and his men watched. They were rooted to the spot, unable to take their eyes off him. At last he pushed his plate away, wiped his lips with his sleeve and sighed, "Ah, that was good! And there was plenty of it too! Your very good health, brothers!" He raised his tankard and drank to the journeymen. "As for you," he advised the Master, "you'd better look more closely before showing strangers the door another time—you can take Big Hat's word for that!"

So saying, he rose, picked up his hatchet and his bundle, and went out of the mill. Krabat and the other men followed him, leaving the Master alone.

Outside, the storm had passed over, the sun shone over the fen, and steam was rising from the ground. The air was fresh as spring water.

Big Hat went on his way without looking back. He crossed the wet meadow, going toward the wood and whistling to himself. Once or twice his gold earring caught the sun.

"Didn't I tell you?" said Andrush. "Those who have dealings with Big Hat don't notice till later what they'd have done better to notice before . . ."

The miller shut himself up in the Black Room for three days and three nights, and his men crept about the house on tiptoe. They had been present when Big Hat defeated the Master in a contest of magic, and they could guess there were bad times ahead.

Their troubles began on the evening of the fourth day. The Master appeared in the servants' hall at supper time and dragged the twelve of them away from their plates. "To work!" He must have been drinking; they could smell it on his breath. He stood there hollow-cheeked, pale as death, his face unshaven.

"What, not in the grinding room yet? Must I help you? Off with you, get the mill grinding, tip in the grain! We'll set all the millstones going, and if there's any dawdling it'll be the worse for you!"

The men had to toil away at their work all night, unmercifully driven by the Master. Shouting and cursing, he chased them back and forth, uttering oaths, threatening punishment, until they were almost fainting. There was not a break all night long, not a moment to draw breath.

When at last day dawned, the men were dropping with exhaustion. They felt as if every bone in their bodies had been broken, and they were all gasping for breath. The Master sent them up to their beds to rest.

He left them in peace all day, but it was the same story

that evening, and so it went on, night after night. As dark fell, the Master would drive them into the grinding room, and they had to slave away to the sound of his jeers and curses until the next day dawned.

Friday night was their only respite, because their Friday evening lessons still went on, though the men were so tired that they could hardly keep awake as they sat on their perch in the shape of ravens, and many of them did fall asleep from weariness.

That did not trouble the Master; what they learned, and how much they learned, was their own affair. It was only once, when Vitko fell off the perch in his sleep, that the Master reproved him.

Vitko, who was still growing, was suffering more than the others, and their nightly drudgery affected him most. Michal and Merten did try to help the boy, and when they could Hanzo, Krabat and Stashko also lent him a hand, but the Master was everywhere, and not much escaped his one eye.

They never spoke of Big Hat, but the men knew the Master was punishing them for witnessing his defeat.

Things went on like this for six weeks, until the first night of the new moon in September. The Goodman with the feather in his hat came driving up as usual, the men set to work, the Master climbed up on the box, picked up the whip and cracked it. In silence, the men ran from the cart to the mill with their sacks, tipped the contents into the hopper above the Dead Stones, and hurried back to the cart. Everything happened as it usually did at the new moon—though it was all rather worse for them—and about two in the morning Vitko could not go on. Carrying one of the last sacks, he began to stagger, and collapsed halfway

between the cart and the mill, where he lay face downward in the grass, gasping for breath. Michal turned him
over and tore his shirt open.

"You there!" The Master jumped up. "What's the meaning of this?"

"How can you ask?" Straightening up, Michal broke the
silence they always observed on nights of the new moon.
"You've made us work like slaves night after night, for six
whole weeks—how could the boy stand it?"

"Quiet!" shouted the Master. He struck out with his
whip; the lash curled around Michal's throat.

"Let be!"

It was the first time Krabat had heard the stranger
speak. His voice was like red-hot coals and bitter frost in
one; Krabat felt it run down his back like an icy shudder,
and at the same time he felt he was standing in the flames
of a blazing fire.

The figure with the plumed hat made a gesture to Michal to take Vitko away. Then he took the whip from the
Master's hand and pushed him down from the cart.

Michal put the boy to bed, and the miller had to work
along with his men instead of Vitko for the rest of the
night, which he usually had to do only between New Year
and Easter—and as for his men, they thought it served
him right.

9 · THE END
OF THE ROW

HE NEXT day the miller left his men in peace, and only the welt on Michal's throat was left to remind them how hard the Master had driven them for weeks, night after night. Now they could go about their work in daylight again, which gave them no trouble to speak of, and they stopped at nightfall, when they could do as they pleased: play the jew's-harp, tell stories, whittle spoons. Everything was the same as before. The blisters on their hands dried up, the sore places on their chests and backs soon healed. When the Master read to them from the Book of Necromancy on Friday evening they were eager to learn again, and learn they did; when he asked questions Juro was usually the only one to get stuck, and that was nothing new.

A few days after Michaelmas the Master sent Petar and Krabat to Hoyerswerda to buy a cask of salt and all sorts of other kitchen stuff. The miller never let one of his men out on his own. If there was something to be done in the outside world, he sent at least two together, and it was to be supposed he had his reasons for that; or else his in-structions.

So the two of them set off at dawn in the rack wagon, with the bays between the shafts. It was misty over the fen, but once they had the wood behind them the sun rose and the mist dispersed. Schwarzkollm lay ahead of them.

Krabat was hoping to catch sight of the singer, and he looked out for her as they drove through the village, but in vain. She was not among the girls standing by the lower well with their buckets, chattering, nor at the upper well, nor was she anywhere else to be seen that morning.

Krabat was sorry; he would have liked to see her again. Easter night was a long time ago.

"Perhaps I will be in luck when we go home this afternoon," he thought. Maybe it would be better not to hope, and then he needn't be disappointed later ...

But as they were going home from Hoyerswerda with their cask of salt and the other things that afternoon, his wish was granted after all. There she was, standing not far from the lower of the two village wells, surrounded by a flock of cackling chickens. She had a basket in her hand, and she was scattering food for them.

"Chick-chick-chick! Chick-chick-chick!"

Krabat recognized her at first glance, and as they drove by he nodded to her, quite casually, because he did not want Petar noticing anything. The girl nodded back, in an equally casual though friendly way, as one nods to a passing stranger, but her mind was on the chickens she was feeding.

There was a fine, speckled rooster among the chickens, busily pecking up the grain at her feet. Just then Krabat envied that rooster with all his heart, and if it had been possible he would have changed places with him on the spot.

The weather was dreary before winter set in that year, chilly and gray, with mist and rain. They used the few dry days to bring in peat, and spent the rest of their time in the mill, the shed and the stable, the granary or the barn. Everyone was glad to have work that would not take him out in the rain.

Vitko had grown a lot since spring, but he was still thin.

"We'll have to put a brick on his head to weigh him down, or he'll be shooting right away from us!" said Andrush, and Stashko suggested fattening him up like a Michaelmas goose. "He needs a bit of flesh on those bones to keep him from looking like a scarecrow!"

The first down was beginning to appear on Vitko's chin and upper lip too—it was red, of course. Vitko did not notice, but Krabat did; watching Vitko, he could see how a boy could grow three years older in a single year of time.

The first snow of the winter fell on St. Andrew's Day, quite late in the year. Once again the journeymen at the mill in the fen grew restless, taciturn and quarrelsome. They would pick a fight at the slightest provocation, and as the weeks went by there were few days when at least one of them did not fly at someone else.

Krabat remembered the conversation he had had with Tonda, about this time last year. Were the men afraid to their very bones because once again one of them was to die?

How had he not come to think of that before? He had seen the Waste Ground, and the row of low mounds, seven or eight of them, perhaps more; he had not counted them. Now he knew why the men were afraid; now he shared their fear! Any one of them, with the possible exception of Vitko, might be the victim this year. But who would it be? And why? Krabat dared not ask any of his companions, not even Michal.

He took out Tonda's knife more often than usual to snap it open and look at the blade. The blade was always shining, so he himself did not seem to be in danger—but it might be different tomorrow.

There was a coffin ready in the woodshed. Krabat discovered it by accident when he went to fetch wood the day before Christmas Eve. It was covered with a piece of canvas, and Krabat would hardly have noticed it but for barking his shins on it in passing.

Who had made that coffin? How long had it been standing there? And who was it for?

That last question left Krabat no peace; it occupied his mind for the rest of the day, and even followed him into his dreams.

Krabat has found a coffin in the woodshed, a pine coffin covered with a piece of canvas. Cautiously, he opens it and looks inside. It is empty.

He decides to chop the coffin up; he cannot bear to think of it standing there, waiting for someone.

Krabat sets to work with his hatchet. He pries the boards apart and splits them from top to bottom. Then he chops them into small, handy pieces, intending to put them in a basket and take them in to Juro.

But as he is looking around for a basket, crack! The coffin has put itself together again. It is intact, all in one piece.

Krabat attacks it with his hatchet for a second time and chops it to matchwood. But no sooner has he done so, than crack!—the coffin is back again.

In a fury now, the young man tries for the third time. He chops and hacks until the splinters fly, until the coffin is nothing but a heap of tiny shavings, but it is no good. Crack! There is the coffin, put together again, without a scratch on it, waiting for its destined occupant.

Horror seizes Krabat. He runs out into the fen. Snow is falling, thick flurries of snow, blinding him. He does not know where he is running to, and he fears the coffin may follow him. After a while he stops to listen.

No sound of wooden feet, no hollow rattling, as he feared. Instead, quite close, there is a grating, scraping sound, like someone digging in stony, frozen ground.

Following the sound, Krabat comes to the Waste Ground, and through the driving snow he makes out a figure digging a hole with spade and pick at the far end of the row of mounds, near the wood—at the very spot where Krabat's one extra flower fell to the ground in summer. Krabat thinks he recognizes the figure. He knows it is one of the miller's men, but he cannot be sure which, in the flurries of snow.

He opens his mouth to call, "Hey! Who are you?"

His voice fails him; he cannot utter a sound, and he finds it impossible to go a step further. He stays where he is. His feet are frozen to the ground, he cannot move them.

"The devil take it!" he thinks. "Have I gone lame? I must take those few steps . . . I must . . . I must . . ."

He breaks out in a sweat as he summons up his last

reserves of strength, but his feet will not obey him. Do
what he will, he cannot move from the spot. And it snows,
and it snows, and gradually the snow covers him up....

Krabat woke bathed in sweat. He threw back the
blanket and tore the clammy shirt from his body. Then he
went to the attic window and looked out.

Christmas Day had dawned. It had snowed overnight,
and he saw a fresh trail of footsteps leading into the fen.

When he went out to wash at the pump Michal came
up the path, with a pick and a spade. He was stooping as
he walked, dragging his feet, and his face was pale. Krabat was about to speak to him, but Michal waved him
away, and indeed, they understood each other without
saying a word.

Michal was a changed man after that. He kept aloof
from Krabat and all the others, even Merten, as if there
were a wall between him and them, as if he were already
far away.

So New Year's Eve came. The Master did not put in an
appearance; he had been gone since morning. Night fell,
and the miller's men went to bed.

Although he had made up his mind to stay awake, Krabat fell asleep like the others. He woke at midnight, and
began to listen.

Somewhere in the house there was a dull thud—then a
scream, and then silence.

Merten, the huge, bearlike, broad-shouldered Merten,
began to sob like a child.

Krabat pulled the blanket up over his ears, dug his fingers into the straw mattress, and wished he were dead.

They found Michal on New Year's Day in the morning. He was lying on the floor of the meal-store; a beam had fallen from the ceiling and broken his neck. They put him on a plank and carried him into the servants' hall, and there they said their farewells to him.

Juro took off his clothes, washed him and laid him in the pine coffin, with a handful of straw under his neck. They took him out to the Waste Ground that afternoon and lowered him into the hole at the far end of the row of mounds, near the wood.

They buried him hastily and did not spend a moment longer than necessary at his graveside.

Only Merten remained behind.

THE
THIRD
YEAR

1 · THE KING
OF THE MOORS

THE MASTER did not reappear for several days, and meanwhile the mill stood still. The miller's men lay on their beds or sat by the warm stove. Had there ever been a journeyman called Michael who worked at the mill in the fen? Even Merten never spoke of him; he never spoke at all, he sat there from morning to night saying nothing. Only once, on the evening of New Year's Day, when Juro brought up the dead man's clothes and laid them at the foot of the empty bed, did he wake out of his trance. He ran out to the barn and hid in the hay until morning. Ever since that he had been utterly listless, seeing and hearing nothing, saying and doing nothing, just sitting about.

These days Krabat's thoughts kept circling around the same tormenting questions. It seemed plain that Tonda and Michal could not both have died by chance, both on New Year's Eve. What game was being played—and who was playing it, and what were the rules?

The miller stayed away until the eve of Twelfth Night. Vitko was just about to blow out the light when the attic door opened, and the Master appeared on the threshold, pale as death. He cast a glance around, but he did not seem to notice Michal's absence. "To work!" he ordered them. Then he turned, and was not seen again that night.

Hastily, the men dressed and hurried downstairs. Petar and Stashko ran to the millpond to open the sluice. The others stumbled into the grinding room, tipped out the grain, and set the mill grinding. It began to go around, rattling and clattering, and the miller's men felt their hearts lift.

"The mill is grinding again," thought Krabat, "and life goes on . . ."

They finished work about midnight, and when they came into the attic they saw someone lying on Michal's old bed, a boy of about fourteen, who looked small for his age. The lad had a sooty face and very red ears. Full of curiosity, the miller's men surrounded him, and Krabat, who was holding the lantern, shone it on him. At that the boy woke, and when he saw the eleven ghosts standing by his bed he was frightened. Krabat felt sure he had seen him before—when could it have been?

"No need to be afraid of us!" he said. "We're the miller's men, and we work here. What's your name?"

"Lobosch. What's yours?"

"I'm Krabat, and this is . . ."

The sooty-faced urchin interrupted him. "Krabat? I once knew someone called Krabat . . ."

"Did you?"

"But he'd be younger than you . . ."

Light dawned on Krabat. "You must be little Lobosch from Maukendorf!" he cried. "And you've blackened your face to play the part of one of the Three Kings from the East!"

"That's right," said Lobosch, "and for the last time too! I'm apprenticed to the miller here now!"

He said this full of pride, and the miller's men kept their thoughts to themselves.

When Lobosch came down to breakfast next morning, he was wearing Michal's clothes. He had tried to scrub the soot off, not entirely successfully; there were still traces around the corners of his eyes and his nose.

"Never mind!" said Andrush. "A morning in the meal-store will clean that off!"

The boy was hungry, and he wolfed down his oatmeal. Krabat, Andrush and Stashko, who were sharing the same dish, were amazed at the amount he could eat.

"If you work as well as you eat the rest of us can take it easy!" said Stashko.

Lobosch looked at him, a question in his eyes. "Ought I to eat less?"

"No, no, eat all you want!" said Krabat. "You'll need all the strength you can get. No one need go hungry here."

But instead of spooning up more oatmeal, Lobosch put his head on one side and studied Krabat, his eyes narrowed.

"Why, you might be his big brother!" he said.

"Whose big brother?"

"That other Krabat's, of course! You remember, I told you I knew someone else called Krabat."

"Whose voice was just breaking, eh? He left you in Gross-Partwitz."

"How do you know?" asked the bewildered Lobosch.

Then he struck his forehead. "What a silly mistake to make!" he cried. "Why, at the time I took you for maybe a year and a half older than me, two years older at the most . . ."

"I am five years older than you," said Krabat.

At that moment the door opened, and in came the Master. The miller's men shrank back from him.

"Hm!" said he, going up to the new apprentice. "You talk too much—you'd better get out of the habit of that." He turned to Krabat, Stashko and Andrush. "He's to eat his breakfast, not chatter! Get that into his head."

And the Master left the servants' hall, shutting the door behind him.

Suddenly Lobosch seemed to have had enough. He put down his spoon, hunched his shoulders, and sat there with his head bent. When he glanced up, Krabat nodded to him across the table—only very slightly, but the boy seemed to understand. He knew that he had a friend at this mill.

Lobosch, in his turn, had to spend a morning in the meal-store. The Master came for him after breakfast.

"Why should he have an easier time than the rest of us?" said Lyshko. "A bit of flour won't hurt him."

Krabat said nothing. He was thinking of Tonda and Michal. If he wanted to help Lobosch he must not make Lyshko suspicious, even over the smallest matters.

Just now there was nothing he could do for the boy. Lobosch would have to get through the morning as best he could, wielding his broom amid clouds of flour dust, his eyelashes stuck together, his nose clogged up. There was no help for that; he must manage somehow. Krabat could hardly wait until Juro called them in to dinner. While the others made their way to the servants' hall, he ran to the meal-store, shot back the bolt and flung the door open. "Come on out—it's midday!" he said.

Lobosch was crouching in a corner, his knees drawn up, his head in his hands. When Krabat called to him, he jumped. Then he came toward the door, slowly, dragging the broom behind him. He jerked a thumb over his shoulder.

"I couldn't do it," he said in a very small voice. "So after a bit I—I just stopped and sat down. Do you—do you think the Master will send me packing?"

"There'll be no reason for him to do any such thing!" said Krabat.

Uttering a magic spell, he traced a pentagram in the air with his left hand. Thereupon the dust in the room rose up, as if the wind were blowing it from every nook and cranny. It sailed out of the door like a plume of white smoke, over Lobosch's head, and away in the direction of the wood.

The room was swept clear. There was not a speck of dust left. The boy opened his eyes wide. "How did you do that?" he asked.

Krabat left the question unanswered. "Promise not to tell a soul!" said he. "Now, let's go in, Lobosch; our soup will be getting cold."

That evening, after the new apprentice had gone to bed, the miller summoned his journeymen and Vitko to his room, and they admitted Vitko to their company just as Krabat had been admitted on Twelfth Night the year before, according to the rules of the mill and the custom of the guild. Hanzo and Petar vouched for Vitko to the Master, and then the red-headed boy was declared free of his indentures. The Master touched his head and shoulders with the blade of the hatchet. "In the name of the guild, Vitko . . ."

Andrus had an empty flour sack waiting in the hall. As soon as the Master dismissed them they popped it over Vitko's head, took the newly made journeyman miller off to the grinding room and there "put him through the mill."

"Gently with him!" Hanzo warned them. "Don't forget how thin he is!"

"Thin or not," said Andrush, "a journeyman miller is no feeble little tailor! He must be able to stand up for himself! Come along, brothers, let's get on with it!"

In accordance with their usual custom, they gave Vitko a thorough working over, but Andrush told them to stop sooner than he had last year, when it was Krabat's turn. Petar took the sack off, Stashko scattered flour over Vitko's head and declared that he had "been through the mill." Then they seized him and tossed him in the air three times, after which he had to drink a toast to them.

"Your health, brother!"

"Here's to you!"

The wine was no worse than usual this Twelfth Night, yet the miller's men could not really manage to feel merry, and that was Merten's doing. He had worked in silence all day, eaten his meals in silence, he stood by in silence while they worked Vitko over, and now he sat on a meal bin, stiff as a post, taking no interest in the proceedings, and there was nothing, nothing at all, that could persuade him to break his silence.

"Hey there!" said Lyshko. "You look as if you had a nasty smell under your nose!" Grinning, he held out a full tankard to him. "Get drunk, why don't you, Merten? Just spare us that glum face of yours!"

Merten got up. Without a word, he went up to Lyshko and struck the tankard out of his hand. The two men stood facing each other, eye to eye. Lyshko began to sweat. The others held their breath.

It was quiet in the room, quiet as the grave. Outside in the passage they heard a soft tapping that hesitated and then came closer. All of them, Merten and Lyshko included, looked at the door, and Krabat, who was nearest to it, opened it.

Lobosch was standing on the threshold, barefoot, in his shirt, a blanket around his shoulders.

"Hello, so it's you, is it, Your Majesty?" said Krabat.

"Yes, it's me. I was frightened, all alone in the attic," said Lobosch. "Aren't you ever coming to bed?"

2·THE WAY YOU FLY WITH WINGS

VERYONE took to young Lobosch, right from the start. Even Merten was kind to him, though he showed it without words, by a nod of the head, a glance or a gesture. Merten was cutting himself off from his companions more and more. He did his work, he went through the day's routine, he did not seem to be sulking, nor did he object to anything the Master or the head journeyman told him to do—but he would not speak. He never spoke at all, not to anyone, and he preserved this silence he had imposed on himself since New Year's Day even on Friday evenings, when the Master read to them from the Book of Necromancy.

The Master was undisturbed. "It's up to you how hard you work to learn the Secret Arts, as you know," he said to his men. "It's all the same to me!"

Krabat worried about Merten, and he felt he ought to try to talk to him. One day soon he, Petar and Merten happened to be sent to the granary to turn the grain. They had hardly started when Hanzo came to fetch Petar away to the stable.

"Carry on by yourselves—I'll send someone else up as soon as there's a man free," said Hanzo.

"Right," said Krabat.

He waited until Hanzo and Petar had left, closing the door behind them. Then, putting his grain shovel down in the corner and placing a hand on Merten's shoulder, he asked, "Do you know what Michal once told me?"

Merten turned to face him.

" 'The dead are dead,' " said Krabat. "He said it twice, and the second time he added, 'Those who die at the mill in the fen of Kosel are forgotten as if they had never been; that's the only way the others can go on living—and life must go on.' "

Merten had listened quietly, and now he took Krabat's hand, which was still lying on his shoulder, removed it in silence, and went on with his work.

Krabat was at a loss. What was he to do about Merten? Tonda would have been able to advise him, perhaps Michal too, but now Krabat was on his own, and it was not so easy.

He was glad Lobosch was there.

The boy fared like all the other apprentices before him, and he could hardly have stood his first few weeks at the mill but for Krabat's help. And Krabat did help him. He knew how to contrive it so that they met from time to time at work; not too often, as if it happened by chance. Then he would stop and exchange a few words with the boy, put a hand on his shoulder, and following Tonda's example, let his own power flow into him. He had learned how to do this one Friday evening. "But mind you don't let anyone notice!" he impressed upon Lobosch. "Take care the Master doesn't learn of it, or Lyshko either. He carries tales to the Master."

"Aren't you allowed to help me?" Lobosch asked. "What if someone finds out?"

"Never mind that," Krabat answered. "The main thing is not to give yourself away."

Young as he was, Lobosch got the point at once. He played his part with considerable skill, and only the two of them knew that he was pretending for the benefit of the others, and things were not really quite so bad as his piti-ful grunts and groans suggested. Every evening he went straight to bed after supper, hardly able to crawl up the attic stairs; every morning, even at breakfast, he looked as tired as if he was about to fall off his chair any moment.

Lobosch was a bright lad, and an excellent playactor, and more besides, as Krabat found two weeks later when he discovered Lobosch hacking away at a great mound of ice behind the mill.

"There's something I wanted to ask you," the boy began. "Will you answer me?"

"If I can," said Krabat.

"You've been helping me since I came to this mill," said Lobosch, "and you've kept on helping me, even though the Master's not to know because he'd be angry with you if he did—that's plain enough, anyone can work that out—"

"Is that what you wanted to ask me about?" Krabat interrupted.

"No, I'm just coming to the question," said Lobosch.

"Well, what is it?"

"How can I pay you back for all your help?"

"Pay me back?" replied Krabat. He was about to dismiss the subject, when he thought better of it. "One day," he said, "I would like to tell you about my friends Tonda and Michal, who are both dead. If you will listen to me then, that will be payment enough!"

About the end of January a thaw set in, as violent as it was unexpected. Only the day before, the fen had been frozen hard; now the west wind was blowing around the house, and had been since the early hours of the morning, far too warm a wind for the time of year. The sun shone, and within a few days most of the snow had melted. A few dirty gray remnants were left here and there, in a ditch or a hollow or the ruts of a cart track, but what were they beside the brown of the fields, the dark of the molehills, the first hint of green under last year's withered grass?

"This is like Eastertide," said the miller's men. As each day passed the warm west wind affected them more and more, making them feel heavy, tired and fidgety. They slept restlessly, dreamed confused dreams and talked in their sleep. Sometimes they would lie awake for hours, tossing on their beds. Only Merten never moved, but lay motionless on his straw matttress, and he did not talk even in his sleep.

Krabat thought about the singer from Schwarzkollm a great deal at this time. He decided he would speak to her at Easter, which was still some time off; however, his mind was full of the thought of where he would go to see her, and how he would stop to talk to her.

These last few nights he had dreamed two or three times that he was on his way to see the girl, but never reached her. Each time something happened to stop him, and later he could not remember what it was.

What *was* it? What was it that stopped him?

He could remember the beginning of the dream quite clearly. He had seized his chance to run away from the mill unobserved. He did not take the usual way to Schwarzkollm, but chose the path across the bog, along which Tonda had once led him on their way home from the peat-cutting. Up to this point everything was clear, and then he could not remember the rest. It tormented him.

One night, as he was lying in bed, wakened by the howling of the wind, he was trying to puzzle it out again. Doggedly he went over the start of the dream in his mind, a third time, a fourth time, a sixth time, until in so doing he fell asleep—and this time he did succeed in dreaming his dream to its end.

Krabat has run away from the mill, seizing his chance to slip out of the house unobserved. He is making for Schwarzkollm to see the singer, but he does not take the usual way; he chooses a path through the bog, the path along which Tonda once led him when they were coming home from the peat-cutting.

Out in the bog he suddenly becomes unsure of himself. Mists have gathered, and he cannot see through them. Hesitantly Krabat gropes his way forward, over quaking ground.

Has he strayed from the path?

He feels the bog sucking at the soles of his feet, he feels himself sink deeper in at every step he takes—to the instep, then to the ankles, then haflway up his calves. He must have wandered into a patch of quicksand. The harder he tries to find his way back to firmer ground, the faster he sinks in.

The bog is cold as death, glutinous, sticky and black. He feels it closing around his knees, his thighs, his hips. Soon he will be entirely swallowed up.

While his chest is still free, he begins to shout for help, though he knows there is not much point in it. Who would hear him out here? Still, he shouts and shouts at the top of his voice. "Help!" he cries. "Save me! I'm sinking, save me!"

The mist has grown thicker, and so it happens that Krabat does not become aware of the two figures until they are within a few paces of him. He thinks he recognizes them as Tonda and Michal.

"Stop!" he cries. "Stay where you are! There's a dangerous patch here."

In the mist the two figures merge into one—how strange! The solitary figure throws him a rope with a piece of wood tied to the end of it. Krabat catches it, clutches the piece of wood, and feels the figure pull him out of the bog and onto firm ground.

It all happens very fast, and now Krabat is standing by his rescuer's side. He tries to thank him.

"Never mind all that," says Juro, and only now does Krabat see that it is Juro who helped him out. "If you want to go to Schwarzkollm another time, you'd do better to fly."

"Fly?" asks Krabat. "How do you mean?"

"Why, the way you fly with wings!"

And that is all the answer Juro makes before the mists swallow him up.

"Fly . . ." thinks Krabat. "The way you fly with

wings . . ." Why did he never think of that for himself?

At once he changes himself into a raven, as he is used to doing every Friday night, spreads his wings and rises into the air. With a few wing-beats he soars up above the mists and makes for Schwarzkollm.

Down in the village the sun is shining, and below him he sees the singing girl standing at the lower of the two village wells, a straw basket in her hand, feeding the chickens. Then a shadow falls across him, he hears the cry of a hawk in his ear, there is a rushing and a whirring, and at the very last moment he turns sharply to the right.

Missing him by a hair's breadth, the hawk pounces on empty air.

Krabat knows his life is at stake. Swift as an arrow, wings spread, he swoops down. He lands beside the girl, scattering the chickens. Once on the ground he turns back to human form. He is safe now!

Blinking, he looks up at the sky. The hawk is gone, vanished—perhaps it has changed course.

Then, suddenly, the Master is standing by the well. He is angry; he stretches out his left hand for Krabat. "Come with me!" he snarls.

"Why?" asks the girl.

"This young man belongs to me!"

"Not so," she says; just two words, but she speaks them in a voice that allows of no question.

Putting her arm around Krabat's shoulders, she wraps him in her shawl of wool. It is soft and warm, like a cloak of safety about him.

"Come," she says. "Come away."

And they walk away together, without a backward glance.

3 · AN ATTEMPTED ESCAPE

HE NEXT morning they found that Merten had disappeared. His bed was stripped, the blankets lay neatly folded at its foot, his working smock and apron hung in the press, his clogs were standing under his stool. No one had seen him go. They did not notice his absence until he failed to come in to breakfast. Baffled, they searched the mill for him, but he was nowhere to be found.

"He's run away!" said Lyshko. "We must tell the Master."

Hanzo barred his way. "That's my job as head journeyman," he said. "Or is that news to you?"

They all expected the Master to fly into a rage when he heard the news of Merten's disappearance, and they were waiting for shouts, curses and imprecations, but nothing of the kind happened.

At dinner Hanzo told the others that the Master seemed to take it lightly. All he had said was, "Merten's crazy!" and when the head journeyman asked what was to be done, he replied, "Let him be. He'll come back of his own accord!" ·

"When he said that he winked," Hanzo told them, "and

that wink was worse than a thousand curses. I turned so cold inside me, I thought I'd freeze to solid ice on the spot. Let's hope Merten's all right!"

"Huh!" snorted Lyshko. "Anyone who runs away from this mill must know what he's in for! Well, Merten has a broad back—broad enough to carry a load of trouble!"

"Oh, do you think so?" asked Juro.

"To be sure I do!" said Lyshko, and he brought his fist down on the table to emphasize his words—whereupon the soup in the bowl splashed up into his face. He let out a yell, for the soup was thick and boiling hot. "Who did that?" cried Lyshko, wiping his eyes and cheeks. "Which of you went and did that?"

One of the other journeymen must obviously be responsible. Stupid Juro was the only one who merely seemed bothered by the waste of good soup.

"Better not bang the table another time, Lyshko!" said he. "Not quite so hard, anyway!"

Merten came back that evening, as dusk was falling, just as Krabat had feared. He stood in the doorway silently, his head bowed.

The Master came out to meet him, in front of all the other journeymen. He was not angry with Merten; instead, he mocked him, asking how he liked his little expedition, and why he was back so soon—didn't he like it in the villages, or what?

"You don't want to tell me, eh, Merten? You haven't opened your mouth for weeks, have you? But I'm not forcing you to speak—you can run away again for all I care. Try it! Try it as often as you like! Only don't set your hopes too high, Merten. You're not the man to do what no one has ever done yet!"

Merten did not flicker an eyelash.

"Well, make believe if you want!" said the Master. "You didn't get away, but *you* don't mind, eh? We know better, I and the eleven of them"—and he pointed to the journeymen and Lobosch—"we all know better! Now, get out!"

Merten crept up to bed.

The miller's men were all unhappy that evening, except for Lyshko. "We must persuade him not to try running away again," said Hanzo.

"You try!" said Stashko. "If you think it will do any good. I don't."

"No," said Krabat. "I doubt if he'll listen."

Overnight the weather changed, and when they went out of doors next morning it was bitterly cold, without a breath of wind. There was ice on the window panes and ice on the rim of the trough under the pump. The puddles around it were covered with ice, the molehills were frozen stiff, and the ground was hard as bone.

"It'll be bad for the winter sowing," said Petar. "No snow, and now this frost . . . a lot of the seed will be spoiled out there in the fields."

Krabat was glad to see Merten appear at breakfast with the others and attack his bowl of oatmeal greedily, obviously making up for yesterday. Then they went to work, and no one noticed Merten slip away from the mill again, this time in broad daylight. It was not until they came in for dinner at noon that they realized he had gone once more.

Merten was away for two days and two nights, longer than any runaway had ever managed before, and they were just beginning to hope he had safely made his escape when he came stumbling across the meadows toward the mill, on the morning of the third day. He was exhausted and blue with cold, and there was a dreadful look on his face.

Krabat and Stashko went to meet him at the door and led him inside. Petar took one of his shoes off, Kito the other, and Hanzo told Juro to bring a bowl of ice-cold water. He put Merten's frozen feet into it and began to rub them.

"We must get him to bed, as quick as we can," said he. "I hope he's going to be all right."

While the men were busy tending Merten, the door opened and the Master came into the room. He stood watching them for a while, but this time he refrained from mocking. He waited until they were about to take Merten upstairs.

"Just a moment!" said he. Going up closer to Merten, he told him, "I think twice should be enough for you, Merten! There is no road for you that leads away from here. You will never escape me!"

That very morning Merten took the third and, as he thought, the final way out.

The miller's men guessed nothing. They had taken him up to the attic, tipped a hot drink down his throat, wrapped him in blankets and put him to bed. Hanzo stayed with him, sitting on the next bed watching until he was convinced Merten had fallen asleep and did not need him anymore. Then he went down to join the others at work.

Stashko and Krabat had been busy for several days dressing the millstones. They had finished four pairs of stones, and today was the turn of the fifth. They were just about to loosen the cramps so as to get at the stones when the door to the grinding room was flung open and Lobosch burst in, white-faced, his eyes wide with terror.

He was gesticulating and shouting; he seemed to be shouting the same thing again and again. The miller's men could not make it out until Hanzo stopped the machinery. It was quiet in the mill then, and only Lobosch's voice could be heard.

"It's Merten! He's hanged himself!" he cried. "Merten's hanged himself. In the barn! Quick—come quick!"

He led them to the place where he had found Merten. Merten was hanging from a beam at the far end of the barn, a halter around his neck, looking as if he were staring at them.

"We must cut him down!" Stashko was the first to realize that Merten was still alive. "Quick! We must cut him down!"

Andrush, Hanzo, Petar and Krabat—everyone who had a knife snapped it open. But none of them could manage to get anywhere near Merten. He seemed to be surrounded by a magic circle. They could take just three steps toward him, but not an inch more; after that their feet seemed to stick to the ground.

Taking the point of his knife between thumb and forefinger, Krabat aimed, threw—and struck the rope.

He hit his mark, but the knife fell to the ground, powerless. Then someone laughed.

The Master had entered the barn. He did not so much as glance at his men, he paid them no more attention than if they were dirt. He bent to pick up the knife and cut the rope. There was a thud. Limp as a sack of grain, the hanged man fell to the ground and lay there at the Master's feet, a rattle in his throat.

"You bungler!"

There was contempt in the Master's voice. He dropped the knife, and spat on the ground in front of Merten.

Every one of the men felt as if the Master had spat at him . . . and they were sure that what he said was meant for all of them.

"I decide who dies at this mill!" cried the Master. "No one else decides for me!"

He went out, and then they could attend to Merten. Hanzo took the noose from his neck, and Petar and Stashko carried him up to bed. Krabat picked up Tonda's knife from the ground. Before putting it back in his pocket, he rubbed the handle carefully with a wisp of straw.

4 · THE WINTER
WHEAT

MERTEN was sick, and he was sick for a long time. He ran a high fever at first, his throat was swollen and his breathing was difficult. He could not swallow a morsel of food for some days, though later he managed to get down a spoonful of soup now and then.

Hanzo had arranged for one of the men to be somewhere near Merten all the time during the day, never letting him out of sight. For some time they kept watch over him by night as well, fearing that in his fever he might try to harm himself again. In his right mind, they all agreed, even Merten would not try the rope again, or indeed try taking his own life by any means at all. The miller had left them in no doubt that there was no escaping from the mill in the fen that way.

"I decide who dies at this mill!" The Master's words were imprinted on Krabat's mind. Weren't they the answer to that question he had been asking himself ever since last New Year's Eve—who was to blame for the deaths of Tonda and Michal?

When he thought it all over, he saw that what he had was still only a clue, no more—but no less either.

At all events, he would have to call the Master to account one day, when everything was cleared up. That, he thought, was as good as decided! Until that time, he must not draw attention to himself. He must act like a good, harmless fellow, an obedient journeyman with no idea of what was going on, yet all the time he must be preparing himself for the day of reckoning, and so he must work doubly hard at his studies in the Secret Arts.

No snow fell these February days, but the frost was as severe as ever. The miller's men had to climb down into the tailrace every morning to hack away the ice, and they kept cursing the cold that had followed the untimely spring weather.

One day soon, about midday, three strangers came out of the wood and walked toward the mill. One of them was tall and strong, a man in the prime of life, while the other two were wrinkled, white-bearded old men.

Lobosch was the first to see them. His eyes were quick, and nothing much escaped them. "We're about to have visitors!" he called to his companions, who were just sitting down to dinner.

They all saw the three men coming along the path from Schwarzkollm. They were dressed like farmers, wrapped in shepherds' cloaks, their winter caps pulled well down on their foreheads.

No farmer from the nearby villages had ever found his way out here to the mill in the fen, not since Krabat had been working there. But these three went right up to the mill and knocked at the door.

Hanzo opened it to them, and the other men crowded into the hall, full of curiosity.

"What do you want?" asked Hanzo.

"We want to speak to the miller."

"I am the miller." Unnoticed by his men, the Master had come out of his room. He went up to the farmers. "Well, what is it?"

The tall man took off his cap.

"We're from Schwarzkollm," he began. "I'm the mayor there, and these are our village elders. We bring you greetings, and we want to ask you to listen to us, miller! It's because of . . . it's . . . I don't suppose you'll be surprised to hear . . . "

The Master cut him short with an impatient gesture.

"Come to the point! What brings you here? No beating about the bush, if you please."

"We want you to help us," said the village mayor.

"How do you mean?"

"This frost, and there's no snow on the fields . . . " The mayor twisted his cap in his hands. "The winter wheat will spoil if we don't have snow soon."

"What has that to do with me?"

"We wanted to ask you to make it snow, miller."

"Make it snow? What gave you that idea?"

"We know that you can do it," said the village mayor. "You can make snow fall."

"And we're not asking you to do it for nothing," one of the old men assured him. "We'll pay you six score eggs, and five geese, and seven chickens."

"You must make the snow fall!" said the other old man. "Or else we'll lose all next year's harvest, and then we'll go hungry . . . "

"And our children too," added the mayor. "Take pity on us, miller—make the snow fall!"

The Master stroked his chin with his thumbnail.

"I've not seen hair nor hide of you in all these years, but now you need me, here you come all of a sudden!"

"You're our last hope," said the village mayor. "If you will not send us snow, we're lost. You can't refuse to help us, miller! We ask you on our bended knees, as if you were the good Lord himself!"

The three of them kneeled down before the Master, bowed their heads and beat their breasts.

"Hear our prayer!" they begged him. "Hear us!"

"No!" The Master spoke sternly, no pity in his voice. "Go back home. What do I care for your winter wheat? I and my men here"—and he pointed to the journeymen—"we won't have to go hungry, not us! I can see to that, and without snow, if need be! As for you, peasants, don't come pestering me with your eggs and your poultry! You can die for all I care, that's your affair. I've no intention of lifting a finger for you and your brood. Come, do you seriously expect it of me ?"

"What about you?" The village mayor turned to the miller's men. "Won't you help us either, kind sirs? Do it—do it, for the sake of God's mercy, for our poor children. We will reward you well!"

"The fellow's crazy!" said Lyshko. "I'll set the dogs on him—hey there!"

He put his fingers to his mouth and gave a shrill whistle, a sound that pierced the listeners to the marrow. The barking of dogs could be heard, many angry dogs, yapping and yowling.

Dropping his cap, the village mayor leaped to his feet. "Come on!" he cried. "They'll tear us to pieces! Run!"

He and the two old men snatched up their shepherds'

cloaks and ran out of the mill, across the meadows, and disappeared into the wood, the same way they had come.

"Well done!" said the Master. "Well done, Lyshko!" He clapped him on the shoulder. "We're well rid of those three—and they won't be back in a hurry, you can be sure!"

Krabat was furious. He felt sorry for the village mayor and his companions. What harm had they ever done the miller, for him to deny them his help? It would have cost him no more than a glance at the Book of Necromancy and the recital of a few words—just those few words necessary in this case, and they were words that Krabat did not know. The Master had not yet taught his men how to make snow fall.

That was a pity, for otherwise Krabat would have helped the farmers himself without a second thought. Petar would probably have done the same, and Hanzo, and a number of the others.

Lyshko was the only one who was glad the miller had turned the farmers away, and proud of his own success in tricking them into thinking there were dogs after them.

However, his glee did not last long. The following night Lyshko suddenly woke with a loud cry, and when the others asked what on earth the matter was, he told them, his teeth chattering with fright, that he had been dreaming of a pack of furious black hounds attacking him, about to tear him in pieces.

"Dear me!" said Juro sympathetically. "What luck it was only a dream!"

That night Lyshko dreamed of the fierce hounds five times more, and five times more he woke screaming, and

wakened the other men. In the end it was more than they
could stand, and they turned him out of the attic.

"Take your blanket, Lyshko, and go off to the barn!"
they told him. "You can dream of hounds all you like
there, and shout yourself hoarse, so long as we don't have
to listen!"

The next morning the men rubbed their eyes and
looked twice before they could believe it. Everything was
white outside. Snow had fallen during the night, and it
was still snowing, big, fleecy snowflakes. They went on
falling halfway through the morning.

The snow would gladden the hearts of the farmers in
Schwarzkollm and the other villages around the fen. Had
the Master relented and helped them after all?

"Maybe Big Hat had a hand in it," said Juro. "The
farmers might have met with him, and I don't suppose
he'd have refused them."

"Big Hat?" said the others. "Why, no, Big Hat wouldn't
have refused them, to be sure."

Yet it could not have been Big Hat after all, for about
midday—and once again it was Lobosch who saw them
coming—about midday the village mayor and the elders
of Schwarzkollm drove up to the mill in a horse sleigh,
bringing the Master what they thought they owed him for
his help: seven chickens, five geese and six score eggs.

"Our thanks to you, miller!" said the mayor, bowing low
to the Master. "Our thanks for taking pity on our children.
You know we're not rich folk, but take what we bring as a
token of our gratitude, and may Heaven reward you!"

The Master heard him out, an expression of annoyance
on his face. The journeymen could see how hard he had to
struggle to keep his self-control as he replied, "*I* don't

know who it was that helped you—it wasn't I, at all events, and let there be no doubt about that! Put that stuff back on your sleigh, and go to the devil!"

With these words he turned his back on the farmers and went into the Black Room, and his men heard him bolt the door on the inside.

There stood the village mayor and his companions with their presents, baffled and dumbfounded.

"Come!" said Juro, helping them reload the sleigh. "You just go back to Schwarzkollm, and when you're home, have a drink or two and forget all about it!"

Krabat watched the sleigh with the three men until it disappeared into the wood, and for a while after that he could still hear the sound of the bells, the crack of the whip, and the voice of the village mayor shouting "Gee up!" to his horses.

5 · MY NAME IS KRABAT

THE SNOW melted, spring came, and Krabat was studying like a man possessed. He had long since outstripped his companions. The Master praised him and showed that he was very pleased with his progress in the Black Art. He did not seem to guess that Krabat was studying and studying and studying so as to be prepared for the day of reckoning.

On the fourth Sunday in Lent, Merten got up for the first time and went to sit in the sun behind the woodshed. He had grown pale and thin, almost transparent, and they could see that his neck was permanently crooked. However, he was speaking again now—just the barest necessities, "yes" and "no," "give me that" or "leave it alone."

On Good Friday they admitted Lobosch to the Black School, and the boy was much surprised when the Master turned him into a raven! He flitted perkily about the room, brushing the skull and the Book with the tips of his wings. The Master had to give the command three times before the young imp would settle on the perch. He was a comical black bird with bright eyes and ruffled feathers.

"This is the way to speak to another in thought, so that

he will hear and understand the words, as if they came from within himself . . . "

The miller's men found it hard to follow the Master that evening; Lobosch kept distracting them. It was amusing to watch him roll his eyes, crane his neck and flap his wings—and never mind what the miller was reading from the Book of Necromancy!

But Krabat did not let a word escape him.

He realized how important this new lesson was, important for himself and the girl from Schwarzkollm. He impressed the spell upon his mind, syllable by syllable, and as he lay in bed, before going to sleep, he repeated it again and again, until he was quite sure he would never forget it.

On Easter Saturday, at dusk, the Master sent his men out again to bring back the sign. When he counted them out, Krabat and Lobosch were left till last, and the miller dismissed them with his dark blessing.

Krabat had put blankets ready in the woodshed, two each, for the sky looked dark as evening came on, and there was a smell of rain in the air. Since they were the last to leave the mill, he urged Lobosch to hurry, in case any of the others might already be on their way to Baumel's End, but when they reached the wooden cross his fears proved groundless.

They collected twigs and pieces of bark from the edge of the wood, and kindled a small fire. Krabat told the boy why they were sitting out here, and how they must spend the night keeping watch by the fire together.

Shivering, Lobosch wrapped himself in his blankets. "A good thing I don't have to sit here on my own," he thought. "I'd probably die of fright, and then maybe they'd have to put another wooden cross up here, a smaller one ... "

Later, they talked about the Black School, and the rules whereby they were instructed in the Magic Arts. Then they were silent for a time, and at last Krabat began to speak of Tonda and Michal.

"I said I would tell you about them one day," he reminded Lobosch. And as he talked to Lobosch about his friends, he realized that he himself was now in Tonda's place, at least so far as this boy opposite him on the other side of the fire was concerned.

At first he did not intend to tell Lobosch anything about the deaths of Michal and Tonda, or at least, no details. But the longer he talked of the two of them, and of Vorshula who lay buried in Seidewinkel churchyard, and how Tonda said that the men who worked at the mill in the fen would always bring a girl bad luck—the longer he talked, the more he felt that the boy had a right to hear what he had meant to spare him. So in the end Krabat told him everything there was to be told, except that he did not mention the secret of his knife blade; he feared that might endanger its magic power.

"Do you know who is guilty of Tonda's and Michal's deaths?" asked Lobosch.

"I have a very good idea," said Krabat. "And if I am proved right, then I'll get even with him."

About midnight a light rain began to fall. Lobosch pulled the blanket over his head.

"Don't do that!" said Krabat. "You won't be able to hear the bells and the singing in the village."

Soon after that they heard the pealing of Easter bells in the distance, and the voice of the singer from Schwarzkollm came over the fields, alternating with the voices of the other girls.

"It sounds pretty," said Lobosch, after a while. "It's worth getting wet to hear that!"

The girls sang, the bells rang out.

Krabat did not even notice when the rain stopped. For him, at this moment, there was neither rain nor wind, warmth nor cold, light nor dark. There was nothing in the world but the singer, her voice and the memory of the way her eyes shone in the light of the Easter candle.

Krabat had decided he would not go out of himself again this time. The Master had taught them the way to speak to another in thought so that he can hear and understand the words as if they came from within himself.

As morning approached, Krabat recited the new spell, directing all the power he could summon up toward the singer, until he believed he could feel that he had reached her. Then he spoke to her.

"There is someone here, begging you to listen to him, singer!" said he. "You don't know him, but he has known you a long time. When you draw the Easter water this morning, fall behind the other girls on the way home. You must walk alone, carrying your pitcher. That someone wishes to meet you in secret, because this concerns only you and him, and no one else in the world."

He repeated this speech earnestly three times, always in the same words. Then day began to break, the singing and the bells fell silent. Now it was time for him to teach Lobosch to draw the pentagram and for them to mark the sign on each other with splinters from the cross. Krabat cut them from the upright with Tonda's knife and charred them in the embers.

Krabat was in a great hurry on the way home, as if he were determined to be the first back at the mill. With his short legs, Lobosch could hardly keep up.

Just before they reached the fen, among the first of the bushes, Krabat stopped. He searched his pockets, then struck his forehead and cried, "I must have left it by the cross!"

"What?" asked Lobosch.

"My knife!"

"The one Tonda gave you?"

"Yes, Tonda's knife."

The boy knew that Tonda's knife was the only keepsake Krabat had of him. "We must turn around and go back for it," said he.

"No, no," said Krabat, hoping that Lobosch would not see through his ruse. "I'll run back alone, it'll be quicker. You'd better sit down here and wait for me."

"If you think so . . . " The boy stifled a yawn.

"Yes, I do."

While Lobosch sat down in the damp grass between the bushes, Krabat hurried back to the spot which, as he knew, the girls would have to pass taking the Easter water home, and hid in the hedge there.

It was not long before they came up the road in a long line, with their pitchers. As they passed Krabat saw that the singer was not among them. So she had heard and understood his request!

When the other girls were all gone, he saw her coming by herself, wrapped tightly in her shawl. He came out of his hiding place and went to meet her.

"My name is Krabat, and I am a journeyman miller. I work at the mill in the fen," he said. "Don't be afraid of me."

The girl looked into his face calmly, as if she had been expecting him.

"I know you," she said. "I have dreamed of you. Of you, and of a man who means you harm—but we took no notice of him, you and I! I have been waiting to meet you ever since, and now you are here."

"Yes, I am here," said Krabat. "But I can't stay long— they expect me back at the mill."

"And I must go home too," said the singer. "Will we meet again?"

Then she dipped an end of her shawl in the pitcher of Easter water, and without a word she wiped the pentagram off Krabat's forehead, quite gently, taking her time, as if it were the most natural thing in the world.

The young man felt as if she had wiped some taint from him. And he was filled with gratitude to her, just for being alive and there with him, looking at him.

6 · LIVING IN
A DREAM

LOBOSCH had dropped off to sleep among the bushes on the outskirts of the wood, and when Krabat woke him he stared at him drowsily. "Did you find it?"

"What?"

"The knife, of course!"

"Oh, the knife—yes," said Krabat. He showed the boy Tonda's knife, snapping out the blade. The blade was black.

"You ought to rub it down and grease it," Lobosch suggested.

"Yes," said Krabat. "Yes. That's what I ought to do."

Then they hurried homeward, meeting Vitko and Juro halfway. They had been at Dead Man's Cross and were late back too.

"I wonder if we'll get there before the rain starts?" said Juro.

As he spoke he looked at Krabat, as if he saw something odd about him.

The pentagram! Krabat's heart lurched. If he came back to the mill without the sign, the Master was bound to be suspicious. Then both he and the girl might be in

danger. Krabat searched his pockets for a piece of charcoal, but he knew there wasn't any there.

"Come on!" Juro urged him. "We'll pay for it if we don't
hurry—let's run!"

At the moment that the young men left the wood and
ran for the mill, the storm broke. A gust of wind tore the
caps from Vitko's and Krabat's heads, and heavy rain beat
down, making Lobosch cry out. By the time they reached
the mill they were all drenched.

The Master was waiting impatiently. They bowed
under the yoke and received his blows on the cheeks.

"Where's the sign, in the devil's name?" he cried.

"The sign?" asked Juro. "Why, there!" And he pointed
to his forehead.

"I can't see anything there!" said the Master.

"Why, then, the rain has washed it off . . . "

The miller hesitated, and seemed to be thinking. Then
he ordered, "Lyshko! Get me a piece of charcoal from the
hearth—and hurry!"

Roughly, he retraced the pentagram on all four foreheads, just above the nose. The touch burned their skin
like fire. "Now, to work!"

They had to toil harder and longer than usual that
morning; it seemed an age to the four of them before the
mark was gone from their foreheads. But at last it was
over, and suddenly little Lobosch found he could lift a
full, heavy sack above his head.

"Hurray!" he cried. "Look how easy it is! Just see how
strong I've grown!"

The miller's men spent the rest of the day celebrating,
eating Easter cakes and drinking wine, singing and danc-

ing. There were tales told, tales of Big Hat among them, and Andrush, getting a little merry, made a speech, the gist of which was that all journeymen were jolly good fellows, and all master millers should be sent to the devil.

"Let's drink to that!" cried he. "Unless anyone here disagrees?"

"No!" they all shouted, raising their tankards, but Stashko protested.

"What—be *sent* to the devil?" he cried. "No, no, Satan can come and fetch away all the master millers for himself! May he wring their necks, every one!"

"Right you are, dear brother!" Andrush embraced him. "Right you are! May the devil fly away with all millers, starting with ours!"

Krabat had chosen a place in the corner, near enough the others for no one to be able to say he wouldn't join in, and yet he was not really one of them. He kept on the edge of the merrymaking, and while the other young men laughed and sang and made boastful speeches, he was thinking of the singer from Schwarzkollm, and how she met him that morning on the way home, and how they stood and talked to each other.

Krabat could remember every word she spoke, every movement and glance of hers, and he could have spent hours sitting in his corner thinking of her, never noticing how time was passing, if Lobosch had not sat down on the bench beside him and nudged him.

"Can I ask you something?"

"Well?" asked Krabat, trying not to sound impatient.

Lobosch was looking worried. "Those things Andrush was just saying, and Stashko! Suppose they come to the Master's ears . . ."

"Oh, as for that," said Krabat, "that's just silly bragging. Couldn't you tell?"

"But the miller!" replied Lobosch. "If Lyshko goes to tell him, what will he do to Andrush and Stashko?"

"He won't do anything to them at all."

"You don't mean that!" cried Lobosch. "He'll never stand for that kind of thing!"

"Why, yes, today he will," said Krabat. "Today we may abuse the Master and wish every kind of plague on him—we may wish him at the devil, as you've just heard, and he won't bear us any ill will today. On the contrary."

"Why not?" asked Lobosch.

"Because if you can get your grievances off your chest once a year," said Krabat, "why, then you'll do what is asked of you all the better for the rest of the time, and as you will find out, a great deal is asked of you at the mill in the fen of Kosel!"

Krabat was no longer the Krabat of former days. For the next few weeks he was living in a kind of dream. He did what had to be done, he talked to the other men, he answered their questions—but really he was far away from all that went on at the mill. He was with the singer, and she with him, and the world around was growing brighter and greener every day.

Never before had Krabat noticed how many kinds of green there were—a hundred varieties of grass green, the green of the birch and willow trees, moss green, here and there a tinge of bluish green, the young, tender green on the banks of the millpond, on every hedge, in every bramble bush, and the dark, muted evergreen of the pines out in the fen, which were often gloomy, even ominous-looking, almost black, yet now and then, especially toward evening, shone as if they were rimmed with gold.

A few times, though not too often, Krabat dreamed of the girl by night as well. The main features of his dream were always the same ...

They are walking together in a wood or a garden, where old trees grow. It is warm summer weather, and the girl wears a pale smock. As they walk among the trees Krabat puts his arm around her shoulders. She bends her head, and he can feel her hair on his cheek. Her kerchief has slipped back on her neck a little, and he wishes she would stop and turn to him, because then he could look into her face. But at the same time he knows it would be better if she does not do so; then no other person could see her face too—no other person who might have the power of sharing his dreams with him.

Krabat's companions noticed that something had happened to change him, and once again it was Lyshko who tried to sound him out. It was the week after Easter. Hanzo had given Krabat and Stashko the job of dressing one of the millstones. They had put it by the door of the grinding room and were busy with their mill bills, deepening the grooves running outward from the middle of the stone. They went carefully, stroke by stroke, so the edges would be sharp. At one point Stashko went away to sharpen his bill, which was blunted, and it took him some time. Lyshko happened to come along with a bundle of empty sacks under his arm. Krabat did not notice him until he stopped and spoke to him; Lyshko always crept about the place quietly, even when there was no need for it.

"Well," said he, with a wink. "What's her name, then? Is she fair, or brown-haired, or dark?"

"Who?" inquired Krabat.

"Why, the girl who's been on your mind so much lately!" said Lyshko. "Do you think we're blind and don't notice that someone's turned your head . . . in a dream, maybe . . . I know a good way to help you meet her. I'm not without experience, you know . . . "

Looking cautiously around, he bent down to Krabat and whispered in his ear, "You have only to tell me her name . . . I could easily arrange it all . . . "

"Oh, be quiet, do!' said Krabat. "I don't know what you're talking about. You're keeping me from my work, you and your foolishness."

Next night Krabat dreamed his now familiar dream of the singer from Schwarzkollm. Again they were walking among the trees, and it was a warm summer's day, but this time they came to an open space in the middle of the wood, and when they began to cross this clearing they had not taken more than a few steps before a shadow fell over them. Krabat flung his coat over the girl's head. "We must get away from here, quick—don't let him see your face!" He pulled the girl back into the shelter of the trees. And he heard the cry of a hawk, shrill, piercing, like a knife going into his heart, and that woke him.

The following evening Krabat was summoned to the Master. He felt ill at ease as he stood before the miller, and saw the Master's one eye fixed upon him.

"I have something to say to you." The miller was sitting

in his armchair like a judge, arms folded, his face stony. "You know that I think the world of you, Krabat," he went on. "You know you can go farther than most of your companions in your mastery of the Secret Arts. Yet lately I have had my doubts. Can I trust you? You have secrets from me—you are hiding something from me! Might it not be wiser to talk to me frankly and answer my questions of your own free will, rather than force me to spy on you? Tell me, now, what's it all about? Then we'll think what to do, in your own best interests. There's still time."

Krabat did not hesitate a moment before answering, "Why, I have no secrets to tell you, Master!"

"Are you quite sure?"

"Quite sure," said Krabat firmly.

"Go, then—and if you find yourself in trouble, don't say I didn't warn you!"

Juro was out in the hall and seemed to have been waiting for Krabat. He drew him into the kitchen and closed the door behind them.

"Here—for you, Krabat . . ."

He pressed an object into Krabat's hand: a small, dried-up root on a loop of plaited thread.

"Take it and hang it around your neck, or you'll dream such dreams as will get you into a very bad way!"

7 · SURPRISES

FOR THE next few days Krabat found the Master remarkably friendly, always giving him preference over his fellow journeymen and praising him for the most ordinary things, as if to show that he was determined not to bear any grudge. Then, one evening about the end of the second week after Easter, they met in the hall of the house while the others were still at supper.

"Ah, Krabat—I'm glad to have a chance to speak to you," said the Master. "There are times when a man's in a bad mood, as you know, and he'll let himself say things he doesn't really mean. In short, that talk we had in my room not long ago—you remember it?—well, that was a stupid business. Unnecessary too, don't you agree?"

The Master did not wait for an answer, but went on in the same breath. "I'd be sorry if you took all I said that evening at its face value! I know you to be a very good fellow, my best pupil for a long time, and unusually reliable—well, you see how I feel!"

Krabat himself was feeling distinctly uncomfortable. What was the Master after?

"Not to beat about the bush any longer," said the Master, "I don't want to leave you in any doubt of my regard for you. I am going to grant you a privilege I have never given any of my pupils before. Next Sunday I'll excuse you from work and give you the day off. You can go out if you like, wherever you fancy; to Maukendorf, or Schwarz-kollm or Seidewinkel, anywhere you please. And so long as you're back by Monday morning, why, that will be good enough for me."

"Go out?" asked Krabat. "What would I do in Mauken-dorf, or some such place?"

"Oh, there are alehouses and taverns in the villages, where you could pass the time pleasantly—and girls to dance with . . . "

"No, no," said Krabat. "I've no fancy for such things. Why should I be treated better than my companions?"

"Why not?" declared the Master. "I see no reason why I shouldn't reward you for your industry and perseverance in your studies of the Secret Arts. You work far harder than anyone else."

The next Sunday morning, when the miller's men were getting ready for work, Krabat prepared to do the same, but Hanzo took him aside.

"I don't know what's up," said he, "but the Master's giving you the day off. I'm to remind you that he doesn't want to see you back at the mill before tomorrow morning, and he says you know about the rest of it."

"Oh, yes," muttered Krabat. "I know about the rest of it sure enough!"

He put on his best coat, and while the other men went to work, as they did every Sunday, he left the house. He sat down on the grass behind the woodshed to think.

The Master had set a trap for him, that was clear, and

now he had to see that he did not fall into it. One thing at least seemed certain; he could go anywhere he pleased but Schwarzkollm. He would have liked best just to stay sitting here behind the woodshed in the sun, idling the day away. But that would look too much as if he guessed the Master's real intentions. "Very well then—Maukendorf let it be!" he thought. "And I'll give Schwarzkollm a very wide berth indeed!"

But perhaps that would be a mistake too. Might it be wiser *not* to bypass Schwarzkollm, but go right through it, that being the shortest way to Maukendorf?

Of course, he must not meet the singer in Schwarzkollm. He would have to take precautions against such a meeting.

He recited his spell, and then spoke to the girl. "Singer, there is something I must ask you," he told her. "I, Krabat, am speaking to you! You must not leave your house today, you must not step outside, whatever happens, and don't look out of the window either. Promise me that!"

Krabat felt sure the girl would do as he asked. Just as he was about to set off, Juro came around the house with an empty log basket.

"Well, you don't seem to be in much of a hurry to get away, Krabat! Do you mind if I sit down here with you for a bit?"

He fished a piece of wood out of his pocket and traced a circle around the place where they were sitting, adding a pentagram and three crosses, as he did on the occasion of their ill-fated horse trading venture.

"I dare say you're thinking that this has nothing to do with gnats and midges!" he remarked.

Krabat admitted he had had his doubts before. "What

you're doing," said he, "is making sure the Master can neither see nor hear us sitting and talking here, however near or far away he is. Am I right?"

"No," said Juro. "He *could* see and hear us, but he won't because he has forgotten us; that is the power of the circle. So long as we keep inside it the Master may think of anything else in the world, but he will not think of you and me."

"Not such a stupid notion," said Krabat, "not so stupid at all . . . " And suddenly, as if he had found the key to a problem, an idea shot through him. He looked at Juro in astonishment. "Then it was you!" he said. "The farmers had you to thank for their fall of snow—and Lyshko for his dream of the fierce hounds! Why, you're not the simpleton we take you for at all, are you? You're only pretending!"

"Suppose I am?" replied Juro. "I won't deny that I'm not quite such a fool as everyone thinks. But as for you, Krabat—now, don't be offended!—you're more of a fool than you have any idea of."

"I am?"

"You still haven't realized just what is going on at this accursed mill! If you did, you'd know better than to study so hard, or at least you'd know better than to show it! Don't you see what danger you are in?"

"Yes," said Krabat. "I have a very good idea."

"You have no idea at all!" Juro told him. Picking a blade of grass, he crushed it between his fingers. "I'll tell you something, Krabat—I've played the part of a fool all these years. But if you carry on as you are now, you'll be the next one at this mill to find out the whole truth. Michal and Tonda and all the others who lie buried out in the

Waste Ground, they all made the same mistake as you. They studied too hard in the Black School, and they let the Master see it. You know now that one of us must die for him every year, on New Year's Eve."

"For the Master?"

"For the Master," said Juro. "He has made a pact with the . . . well, let us say with the Goodman. Every year he must sacrifice one of his pupils to him, or else he will be taken himself."

"How do you know this?"

"I have eyes in my head, and I can make sense of what I see. And then I've read the Book of Necromancy."

"What, you?"

"I'm a fool, as you know—or as the Master and everyone else knows! They think me simple, only good enough for the housework. I have to clean and scrub and dust— and sometimes I have to clean the Black Room, and there the Book lies, chained to the table, safe from anyone who could read it. The Master wouldn't like any of us to read it . . . there is much in that Book that could harm him if we were to learn it."

"So you *can* read!" said Krabat.

"Yes," said Juro, "and you are the first and only person I have told. Now there's one way, only one, to get the better of the Master: if you know a girl who loves you, she could save you. If she will ask the Master to let you go, and if she can pass the test he will give her."

"Test?"

"I'll tell you about it another day, when we have more time," said Juro. "For the moment, there's only one thing you need know: make sure you don't let the Master know who the girl is, or it will be Tonda's story all over again."

"Do you mean Vorshula?"

"I do," said Juro. "The Master learned her name too soon, and then he tormented her in her dreams until she drowned herself in her despair."

He pulled up another blade of grass and crushed it.

"Tonda found her the next morning. He carried her home to her parents' house and laid her down at the door. It was after that his hair went gray. His strength was all gone—and you know the end of his story."

Krabat imagined himself finding the girl from Schwarzkollm drowned one morning, waterweeds in her hair.

"What am I to do? Tell me!" he asked.

"What are you to do?" Juro picked a third blade of grass. "Go off to Maukendorf, or anywhere else you like— and try to lead the Master astray as well as ever you can!"

As he walked through Schwarzkollm Krabat looked neither to left nor to right. The girl kept out of sight. He wondered what she had told her family to explain why she was staying indoors.

Krabat turned into the village alehouse for a short rest, ate a piece of black bread and some smoked meat and drank a glass of spirits. Then he went on to Maukendorf, sat down at a table in the tavern there and called for beer.

That evening he danced with the girls, talked nonsense to them, turned their heads and picked a quarrel with the local lads.

"Get out of here, you!" they cried.

When they grew really angry and were about to throw

him out by force, he snapped his fingers, and there they were, rooted to the spot, unable to move.

"You silly sheep!" said Krabat. "So you thought you'd set about me? You'd better fight each other!"

At that, such a brawl broke out on the dancing floor as Maukendorf had never seen. Tankards flew through the air, chairs were broken. The young men fought as if they were out of their minds, attacking each other blindly. The landlord wrung his hands, the girls screeched, and the musicians jumped out of the window to save their own skins.

"Good, very good indeed!" Krabat encouraged the young men. "Excellent! Give yourselves a good hiding! Keep it up, now, keep going, and it ought to last you some time!"

8 · A HARD TASK

HE NEXT morning the Master asked where Krabat had been on Sunday, and how he had enjoyed his day out.

"Oh, pretty well!" said Krabat, shrugging his shoulders. Then he told the Master about his visit to Maukendorf, the dancing there and the fight with the village lads. It was good fun, he said, but it would have been far more amusing if he'd had a companion —Stashko, maybe, or Andrush, or indeed any of the others.

"Lyshko, say?"

"No, not Lyshko," said Krabat, risking the Master's displeasure.

"Why not?"

"I can't stand him," said Krabat.

"You too?" The Master laughed. "Then we feel the same about Lyshko. Are you surprised to hear that?"

"Yes," said Krabat. "Yes, I *am* surprised."

The Master looked him up and down. His glance seemed friendly, though there was some mockery in it.

"That's what I like about you, Krabat—you're an honest fellow, you always tell me what you think straight out!"

Krabat avoided meeting the Master's eye. He did not know if he meant what he said; it could equally well be a veiled threat. At all events, he was glad when the miller changed the subject.

"As for what you were saying just now about taking a companion—remember this, Krabat! From now on you can go out on Sundays when you like, or you can stay at home if you prefer. But I am granting this privilege only to you, as my best pupil, and that's my last word."

Krabat was impatient for a private talk with Juro; Juro, on the other hand, had been avoiding him since their meeting behind the woodshed on Sunday. Krabat would dearly have liked at least to communicate with him in thought, but that particular spell did not work within the Secret Brotherhood.

When at last they did meet, in the kitchen, Juro informed Krabat that he must wait a few days "for that knife you gave me to sharpen. I'll let you have it when it's ready. I haven't forgotten."

"Very well," said Krabat. He understood Juro's true meaning.

Half a week went by, and then the Master had to go away again. Before he set off he told his men he would be away for two or three days.

The following night Krabat was wakened by Juro.

"Come into the kitchen; we can talk there."

"What about them?" Krabat pointed to their companions.

"They're so fast asleep a thunderstorm wouldn't wake them," Juro assured him. "I've taken care of that."

In the kitchen, Juro drew the magic circle with its pentagram and crosses around the table and chairs, and lit a candle, which he placed between himself and Krabat.

"I've been keeping you waiting on purpose," he began. "No one must guess that we are meeting in secret. I told you certain things last Sunday, and I dare say you've been thinking them over."

"Yes," said Krabat. "You were going to show me a way to escape the Master; and if I understood you correctly, it's a way I can avenge Tonda and Michal too."

"It is," Juro told him. "If you have a girl who loves you, she can come to the Master on the last night of the year and ask him to let you go free. If she passes the test he will put her to, then he himself must die on New Year's Eve."

"Is the test hard?" asked Krabat.

"The girl must prove that she knows you," said Juro. "She must pick you out from your companions and say, 'This is the man.'"

"And then?"

"That's all that is laid down in the Book of Necromancy, and to read it or hear it, you'd think it was child's play."

Krabat agreed—unless there was a catch in it. He reserved judgment. Was there a secret phrase in the Book, for example? The directions might contain a hidden double meaning . . . if he only knew just how the words ran . . .

"The words are clear and plain," Juro assured him, "but the Master interprets them in his own way."

He reached for the candle snuffers and trimmed the smoking wick.

"Years ago, when I was still quite new here, there was a journeyman among us, one Janko, who tried to do it. His girl turned up on time, on the last evening of the year, and asked the miller for his freedom. 'Very well,' said the Master, 'if you can pick out Janko, he is free and you can take him with you, as it is written.' Then he led her into the Black Room, where the twelve of us were sitting on the perch in the shape of ravens. He made us all put our beaks under our left wings. So there we perched, and the girl was quite unable to tell which was Janko. 'Well?' the Master asked her, 'is it this one, on the extreme right, or that one there in the middle, or one of the others? Take your time, think it over; you know what depends on it.' Yes, the girl said, she knew. And so, after hesitating for some time, she pointed to one of us at random—and it turned out to be Kito."

"And then?" asked Krabat.

"Neither Janko nor the girl lived to see New Year's Day," said Juro.

"And since then?"

"Tonda was the only one who once meant to try the test, with Vorshula's help—but you know about that."

The candle was smoking again, and once more Juro trimmed the wick.

"There's one thing I still don't understand," said Krabat, after a long silence. "Why has no one else ever tried to escape this way?"

"Most of the others don't know about it," Juro replied, "and the few who do hope from year to year that they will not be harmed. There are twelve of us, and death comes to only one every New Year's Eve. And there's something more at stake, which I ought to tell you about. Suppose a girl passes the test, and the Master's power is overthrown.

At the moment of his death all he ever taught us will be gone. At a blow we'll be ordinary journeyman millers again, and the magic-making will all be over."

"Wouldn't that happen if the Master were to die some other way?"

"No," said Juro, "and that's another reason why the few who know it put up with the death of one of their companions every year."

"But you!" said Krabat. "Haven't you done anything about it yourself?"

"I did not dare," said Juro. "And I have no girl to come and ask for my freedom."

He was playing with the candlestick, holding it in both hands, pushing it back and forth on the table slowly, looking at it as if by so doing he were trying to find out something important.

"Let's understand each other," said he, at last. "You needn't make any decision yet, Krabat, or not a final one. But now, at once, we ought to begin to do everything in our power to see that you can make the test easier for the girl, if need be!"

"I can!" said Krabat. "I'll tell her what she needs to know in her thoughts—*that* will work, we've just learned to do it!"

"No, it won't work then," Juro told him.

"Why not?"

"The Master has the power to stop it. He did so with Janko, and he'll do so again, no doubt about that."

"What, then?" asked Krabat.

"During these next months," said Juro, "you must try to reach a point where you can oppose the Master's will. When we are on our perch in the shape of ravens, and he orders us to put our beaks under our left wings, you must be the only one who can put your beak under your right wing. If you can act differently from us during the test, you'll show who you are, the girl will know which raven to point to, and then you'll have won."

"What can we do, then?" asked Krabat.

"Train your will."

"Is that all?"

"More than enough, as you'll find out. Would you like to begin now?"

Krabat said he would.

"Let's suppose that I am the Master," said Juro. "When I give you an order, you try to do the opposite of what I say. Suppose I ask you to move something from right to left, you move it from left to right. When you're told to stand up, you sit where you are. If I order you to look me in the face, you look away. Is that clear?"

"Quite clear," said Krabat.

"Good—then let's begin." Juro pointed to the candlestick on the table between them. "Take hold of that," he said, "and move it closer to you."

Krabat put out his hand to the candlestick, with the firm intention of pushing it away from him and toward Juro—but he met with sudden opposition. A strong power reached out to him, working against the power of his own will, and for a moment he was quite paralyzed by it. Then a silent duel broke out between them. On one side was Juro's will, and on the other Krabat's, trying to oppose it, to bend and break its power.

He was still determined to push the candlestick away. "*Away* from me!" he thought. "Away . . . away."

But he felt Juro's will gradually taking over and extinguishing his own.

"As . . . as you wish," Krabat heard himself say at last.

And he drew the candlestick obediently toward him. He felt utterly empty and drained. If anyone had told him at that moment that he was now dead, he would have believed it.

"Don't give up hope!"

He heard Juro's voice from very far away. Then he felt his friend place a hand on his shoulder, and again, quite close this time, he heard Juro speak.

"That was only your first attempt, remember, Krabat!"

After that they spent every night the Master was out of the house in the kitchen. Taught by Juro, Krabat was training himself to set his own will against his friend's. It was a hard task for both of them, and often Krabat was near despair. "I'll never do it," he cried, "And if I'm to die anyway, at least I don't want her death on my conscience too! Can't you see that?"

"Yes, I see that, Krabat," said Juro. "But she is not involved yet. You needn't worry which way you'll decide yet. It's more important for us to make progress. If you don't lose heart and give up, you'll see how well we'll be doing by the end of the year, believe me!"

Once again—how many times was it now?—they set grimly to work. And gradually, late in the summer, Krabat began to succeed now and then.

9 · THE SULTAN'S EAGLE

AS THE Master suspicious of Krabat and Juro? Was he on their track, with Lyshko's help maybe? One evening early in September he invited his journeymen to drink with him, and when they were gathered around the big table in his room, and every tankard was full, he unexpectedly announced, "A toast to friendship!" Juro and Krabat, taken aback, exchanged glances across the table.

"Drink up!" cried the Master. "Drink up, all of you!" Then, telling Lobosch to refill the tankards, he said, "Last summer I told you about my best friend, Jirko, and I told you too that it was I who brought him to his death. Now I will tell you how it happened: It was at the time of the great war against the Turks. Jirko and I had had to leave Lusatia for a while, and so we parted. I enlisted as a musketeer in the Emperor's army, while Jirko, unknown to me, hired himself out to the Turkish Sultan as a magician. The Marshal of Saxony was in command of the Imperial Army, and he had led us far into Hungary. We were facing the Turkish army, friend and foe both entrenched in fortified camps, and for weeks on end we would hardly have known a war was going on, but for the occasional skirmishing of raiding parties from both sides, and the firing of cannon into the no man's land between us, to find their range. Then one morning it turned out that the Turks had kidnaped the Marshal of Saxony in the night and carried him off, obviously with the aid of magic. Soon after that a Turk came riding out to our trenches to negotiate. He said the Marshal was a prisoner in the hands of the Sultan, and if our army would withdraw from Hungary within six days he would be set free; if not, he was to be strangled on the morning of the seventh day. There was great consternation, and not knowing that Jirko was in the Turkish camp I volunteered to go and fetch the Marshal back."

The Master emptied his tankard at a draught, signed to Lobosch to pour more wine, and went on.

"Our captain said I was out of my mind, but he passed my offer on to the colonel, who took me to see a general, and this man took me before the Duke of Leuchtenberg, who had taken the command in the Marshal's place. At first the Duke did not believe in me either, but then I turned his staff officers into parrots before his very eyes, and I changed the general into a golden pheasant. At that the Duke changed his tune. He told me to turn his officers back again at once, and promised me a reward of a thousand ducats if I succeeded in rescuing the Marshal. Then he had his own riding horses brought out for me, and told me to choose myself one."

Once more the Master paused to drink, and once more Lobosch refilled his tankard before he continued.

"Now," said he, "I might simply go on with my story . . . but I have a better notion. You can live out the rest of the story for yourselves! Krabat will play my own part—the part of a musketeer skilled in magic, who is going to rescue the Marshal of Saxony. Now we need someone to be Jirko . . ."

He glanced from one of his men to another, looking Hanzo over, considering Andrush and Stashko, and at last his eyes rested on Juro.

"You'll do," said he. "You may play Jirko if you like."

"Very well," said Juro, shrugging. "I suppose someone has to do it."

Krabat was not deceived by his friend's foolish grin. It was clear to them both that the master intended to test them in some way, and now it was important to be on their guard and not betray themselves.

The miller crumbled some dried herbs over the candle flame, and a heavy, druglike fume spread around the room. The miller's men felt their eyelids droop heavily.

"Close your eyes!" the Master told them. "Then you will see what happened in Hungary, while Juro and Krabat act out the story—the story of myself and Jirko in the great Turkish war . . ."

Krabat felt weariness overcome him, felt himself slowly falling asleep as he heard the Master's voice, monotonous and far away.

"Juro, the Sultan's magician, is in the Turkish camp. He has sworn allegiance to the crescent of Islam. And there is Krabat, Krabat the musketeer, in his white gaiters and blue coat, standing at the Duke of Leuchtenberg's right hand, inspecting the parade of horses . . ."

Krabat, Krabat the musketeer, in his white gaiters and blue coat, is standing at the Duke of Leuchtenberg's right hand, inspecting the parade of horses. He likes the look of a black horse with a tiny white mark on the forehead; from a distance the mark looks like a pentagram.

"I'll take that one!" he says.

The Duke has the black horse saddled and bridled for him. Krabat loads his rifle, hangs it over his shoulder, and mounts. He trots gently around the parade ground, then puts spurs to the horse, and gallops toward the Duke and his retinue as if he intended to ride them down.

The officers scatter in alarm—but Krabat sweeps over their powdered white heads, and to their amazement they see the horse carry him straight up into the air. And that is not all. Horse and rider begin to disappear, dissolving gradually into thin air until they finally vanish from sight completely, even from the sight of the Master of the Ordnance, Baron Gallas, who has the best telescope in the Imperial Army at his disposal.

Krabat rides up and up to dizzy heights, as other men might ride over a level plain. Soon he catches sight of the first Turks on the outskirts of a bullet-riddled village. He sees their turbans, bright in the sun, he sees the cannon in position behind their gabions, he sees patrols riding back and forth between the outposts. He himself, however, and his horse, are invisible. The Turkish horses blow out their nostrils with fear as he passes, the dogs begin to howl and put their tails between their legs.

The green banner of the Prophet is waving in the wind above the Turkish camp. Krabat guides his horse carefully down to earth. Not far from the magnificent tent which houses the Sultan he sees another, rather smaller tent, guarded by some twenty janissaries, all armed to the teeth.

Leading his horse, he enters the tent. Sure enough, there is that great warrior-hero the Marshal of Saxony, the scourge of the Turks, seated on a stool, his head in his hands. Krabat makes himself visible, clears his throat, goes up to the Marshal—and steps back in amazement.

The Marshal is wearing a black leather patch over his left eye!

"What is it?" he asks Krabat in a hoarse voice, a voice like a raven croaking. "Are you in the service of the Turks? How did you get into this tent?"

"I am at your service, sir!" says Krabat. "My orders are to rescue Your Excellency. My horse is ready!"

And the horse too becomes visible.

"If your Excellency has no objection . . ." says Krabat.

He swings himself up on the horse, signing to the Marshal to get up behind. Then they break out of the tent.

The janissaries are so surprised that they do not lift a finger, and shouting boldly "Make way there!" Krabat and the Marshal race through the middle of the camp. At the sight of them even the Sultan's Nubian guards drop their spears and swords.

"Hurrah!" shouts Krabat. "Hold tight, your Excellency!"

No one dares to bar their way, and already they are at the gates of the camp. They ride out into open country. Then Krabat makes the horse rise in the air. Only now do the Turks begin to fire at them, volleys of shots, and the bullets whistle in the air around them.

Krabat is in a cheerful mood. He does not fear the Turkish bullets.

"If those fellows were going to hit us, they'd have to shoot with something made of gold!" he tells the aston-

ished Marshal. "Bullets of iron and lead will do us no harm—or arrows either!"

The shots die away, the firing stops. Then the two riders hear a rushing and a roaring sound, coming from the Turkish camp and swiftly getting closer. Krabat cannot turn around as they ride through the air, so he asks his companion to look behind them.

The Marshal says he sees a huge black eagle following them. "He is swooping down from high above, the sun at his back, his beak toward us!"

Krabat recites a magic spell, and great clouds tower up between them and the eagle, thick, gray clouds, like a misty mountain range.

The eagle plunges on, right through them.

"There!" croaks the Marshal. "It's swooping down on us."

By now Krabat knows what kind of an eagle it is following them, and he is not surprised when the eagle cries out in human language.

"Turn back!" calls the eagle. "Turn back, or you are dead men!"

Krabat knows that voice. Where has he heard it before? No time to wonder about that! He makes a sign, and a storm breaks around them, flinging the eagle back, a storm that should sweep him right out of the sky. But it fails. The Sultan's eagle is a match for any storm.

"Turn back!" he calls. "Surrender, before it is too late!"

"That voice!" thinks Krabat. He recognizes it now. It is the voice of Juro, Juro who was his friend when they were journeyman millers together, many years ago, at the mill in the fen of Kosel.

"The eagle!" the Marshal warns him. "He's nearly caught up with us!"

Suddenly Krabat recognizes the voice croaking in his ear as well. "Your gun, musketeer!" it is urging him. "Fire! Why don't you shoot the monster down?"

"Because I have nothing made of gold!" Krabat is glad; it is true, too. But the Marshal of Saxony—or whoever it may be sitting there behind him—the Marshal tears a golden button off his coat.

"Put that in your gun—now, fire!"

Juro, Juro the eagle, is only a few wing-beats away now. Krabat has no intention of killing him. He pretends to be putting the golden button in the barrel of his rifle, but in fact he lets it slip from his hand.

"Fire!" the Marshal insists. "Fire!"

Without turning his head, Krabat fires the gun over his left shoulder at their pursuer; it is blank, as he knows, loaded only with powder, no golden button in the barrel.

There is the sudden crack of a shot—and a shriek of agony.

"Krabat! Kra-baa-aaht!"

Horrified, Krabat drops his gun. He covers his face with his hands and weeps.

"Krabat!" someone is calling in his ear. "Kra-baa-aaht!"

Krabat woke, with a moan. How did he come to be sitting here at the table, with Andrush and Petar and Merten and all the others? They were staring at him, white, appalled, and each man looked away as soon as he felt Krabat's eyes on him.

The Master sat in his place, still as a corpse, leaning

back in his chair, as if he were listening to something far away.

Juro was motionless too, lying with the upper half of his body over the table, face down, his arms spread wide—arms that had been eagle's pinions beating strongly only a few moments ago. There was a spilled tankard beside him, and a dark red spot on the table top . . . was it wine or blood?

Lobosch threw himself on Juro, sobbing. "He's dead, he's dead!" he cried. "You killed him, Krabat!"

Feeling his gorge rise, Krabat tore his shirt open with both hands.

Then he saw Juro move first one arm, then the other. Slowly, as it seemed, life was coming back into his body. Propping himself on his hands, Juro raised his face. There was a round red mark on his forehead, just above his nose.

"Juro!" Little Lobosch grasped his shoulders. "You're alive, Juro, you're still alive!"

"Why, what else?" inquired Juro. "It was only done in play . . . but my head was fairly ringing with that shot of Krabat's! Someone else can play the part of this Jirko another time! I've had enough—I'm off to bed!"

The miller's men laughed aloud in relief, and Andrush said what they were all thinking. "Yes, you go to bed, brother! Thank heaven you're all right."

Krabat sat at the table as if turned to stone. The shot, the scream, and now this light-hearted merriment all of a sudden . . . how did it all fit together?

"Stop!" the Master interrupted them harshly. "Stop it! I can't stand it! Sit down and be quiet!" He had risen and was leaning one hand on the table; his other hand was clasped around his tankard as tightly as if he would crush it to pieces.

"Yes," he cried, "what you saw was only a nightmare! You wake from a nightmare, and then . . . But I didn't dream the story of Jirko, that time when I was in Hungary. I *did* shoot him! I killed my friend, I *had* to kill my friend—as Krabat did, as every man of you would have done in my place, every single one!"

He brought his fist down on the table, making the tankards dance, reached for the jug of wine and drank from it greedily. Then he flung it at the wall, shouting, "Get out! Go away, all of you, get out of here! I want to be alone—alone—alone!"

Krabat wanted to be alone, too, and he slipped out of the mill. There was no moon that night, but there was starlight. He walked through the wet meadows to the millpond, and when he looked down at the black water, from which the stars sparkled up at him, he felt a longing to bathe in it. Taking off his clothes, he slid into the pond and swam a few strokes out from the bank.

The water was cold and cleared his head, which was what he needed after all that had happened that evening. He went under and surfaced again a dozen times, and then, gasping and with chattering teeth, turned back to the bank.

Juro was standing there with a blanket.

"You'll catch cold, Krabat! Come on out—what are you doing?"

He helped Krabat back on land, wrapped the blanket around him and began to rub him dry.

Krabat pulled away from him. "I don't understand it, Juro!" he said. "I don't see how I *could* have shot at you!"

"You didn't shoot at me, Krabat—not with the golden button."

"You know that?"

"I know what would happen—I know you!" Juro nudged him in the ribs. "A shriek like that may sound nasty, but it's no great effort to produce one!"

"What about the mark on your forehead?" asked Krabat.

"Oh, that!" said Juro, smiling. "Don't forget, I know a little of the Secret Arts . . . just enough for my purposes!"

10 · A RING OF HAIR

URING the summer Krabat had made use of his privilege of going out on Sundays a few times, less for his own amusement than to give the Master no grounds for suspicion. Yet he could not get rid of his feeling that the miller was still planning to trick him. Three weeks had gone by since he shot at Juro, and during that time the Master had hardly exchanged a word with Krabat. Then one evening he mentioned casually, as if it were nothing of importance, "I suppose you'll be off to Schwarzkollm next Sunday, eh?"

"Schwarzkollm? Why?" asked Krabat.

"There's a fair there next Sunday. I'd have thought you'd want to go."

"Oh, I'll see," said Krabat. "You know I don't much care for mixing with strangers when I don't have any of my friends with me."

Later he asked Juro what he ought to do.

"Go, of course," said Juro. "What else?"

"It's a lot to ask," said Krabat.

"Well, there's a lot at stake," said Juro. "Besides, it would be a good chance for you to talk to the girl."

Krabat was surprised. "You mean you know she lives in Schwarzkollm?"

"I've known that ever since we sat by the Easter fire. It wasn't hard to guess."

"Then you know who she is?"

"No," said Juro, "and I don't want to know either. No one can make me tell what I don't know."

"But if I meet her," said Krabat, "how can we keep it from the Master?"

"You know how to draw the magic circle," said Juro, and putting his hand in his pocket, he gave Krabat a piece of charcoal. "Take it—go and meet your girl, and talk to her!"

Krabat went to bed early on Saturday. He wanted to be alone, to make up his mind whether to meet the singer from Schwarzkollm. Dare he tell her the whole story now?

Recently he had managed to win his struggles of will power with Juro more and more often; indeed, sometimes Juro would break out in a sweat first. Not that that was saying much, Juro remarked, and Krabat must not on any account make the mistake of underestimating the Master. But on the whole, things looked quite hopeful.

Krabat felt more confident every time he won. After all, Big Hat had defeated the miller; why couldn't he do the same? He could rely on Juro's help—and on the girl from Schwarzkollm.

But it was on this very point that Krabat was still in doubt. Ought he to involve the girl in his affairs? Who gave him any right to do so? Was his life worth the risk of hers?

Krabat was undecided. He had to agree with Juro that it was a good chance to meet her, and who knew when he would get another? If only it were not for his uncertainty!

Was he to tell her everything tomorrow, when he had not made up his own mind yet?

"Suppose I tell her most of it?" he thought suddenly. "Everything but the day and the hour of the test. . . ?"

He felt great relief.

"That will mean she needn't make a decision at once, and for me it will mean a respite. I can wait and see how things go. I can wait until the very last moment, if need be."

Krabat's fellow journeymen envied him when, after dinner on Sunday, he said the miller had given him the rest of the day off to go to the fair in Schwarzkollm.

"A fair!" cried Lobosch. "Just hearing the word makes me think I see huge plates of cakes before my eyes, and mountains of sweet pastries! Bring me home something nice to eat, do!"

Krabat was about to say, "Of course!" but Lyshko got in first and asked what Lobosch was thinking of. "Do you suppose Krabat has nothing better to do in Schwarzkollm than think about cakes?"

"No!" said Lobosch. "What better things *are* there to think about at a fair?"

He spoke with such deep feeling that everyone had to laugh. Krabat asked Juro for one of the napkins in which they carried food when they went out to work in the wood or at the peat-cutting, folded it up and put it under his cap, saying, "Wait and see what there is for you, Lobosch!"

He strolled out of the house, crossed the fen, and once on the other side of the wood he took the path through the fields that led past Schwarzkollm. He drew the magic circle and sat down inside it at the spot where he had met the girl on Easter morning. The sun was shining, and it was pleasantly warm for the time of year—good weather for a fair! Krabat looked across to the village. In the orchards, the fruit was already picked, but a dozen forgotten apples showed yellow and red among the withered leaves.

He recited his spell in an undertone, directing all his thoughts toward the singer.

"There is someone sitting here in the grass, someone who wants to talk to you!" he told her. "Give him a little of your time—he promises it will not take long. No one must know where you are going or whom you are meeting; he asks you that, and he hopes you can come."

He knew he would have to wait for a while, and he lay down on his back, his arms folded behind his head, to think over what he was going to say to her again. The sky was a clear blue high above him, and as he gazed up at it Krabat's eyelids grew heavy.

When he woke, the girl was sitting on the grass beside him. At first he could not think what she was doing sitting there, patiently waiting, in her pleated Sunday skirt, a bright silk shawl printed with flowers around her shoulders, her hair covered by a lace-edged white linen cap.

"Have you been here long, singer?" he asked. "Why didn't you wake me?"

"I have time to spare," she said, "and I thought it would be best to let you sleep."

He leaned up on his right elbow. "It's a long time since we saw each other," he began.

"Yes, it is a long time." The girl pulled at the ends of her shawl. "But you have sometimes been with me in my

dreams. We were walking under some trees—do you remember that?"

Krabat laughed a little.

"Yes, under the trees!" said he. "It was summer, and the
weather was warm, and you were wearing a light
smock . . . I remember it as if it were yesterday."

"And so do I." The singer nodded and turned to look at
him. "Why did you want to talk to me?"

"Why, I almost forgot!" said Krabat. "Singer, if you
wanted, you could save my life . . ."

"Save your life?" she asked.

"Yes," said Krabat.

"How?"

"I can tell you quickly enough."

Then he told her about the danger he was in, and how
she could help him, provided she could pick him out from
the other ravens.

"With your help that ought not to be hard," said she.

"Hard or not," Krabat warned her, "you must be quite
clear that if you do not pass the test you lose your own
life."

The girl did not hesitate for a moment. "I would will-
ingly give my life for yours," she said. "When must I go to
the miller to ask for your freedom?"

"I'd rather not tell you that today," said Krabat. "Not
yet. I will send you word when the time comes—I'll send
a message by a friend if need be."

He asked her to describe the house where she lived. She
did so, and asked if he had a knife with him.

"Here you are," said Krabat.

He gave her Tonda's knife; the blade was black, as it
always was these days, but it brightened again when the

girl held it in her hands. She untied her cap and cut a lock of her hair, twisted it into a narrow ring and gave it to Krabat.

"This will be our token," said she. "If your friend brings it with him, I will be sure he comes from you."

"Thank you." Krabat put the ring of hair into the pocket of his smock. "Now you must go back to Schwarzkollm, and I'll follow you," he said. "And remember, we mustn't seem to know one another at the fair."

"Does 'not know' mean not dance together?" she asked.

"Not exactly!" said Krabat. "But not too often—you understand that?"

"Yes, I understand."

So saying, the girl rose to her feet, smoothed the pleats of her skirt and went back to Schwarzkollm, where the musicians were already striking up the music for the fair.

There were tables and benches placed outside the village hall to form a square around the dancing floor, where the young people were already twirling around when Krabat arrived. The old folks sat sedately watching the girls and young men. The older men were smoking pipes, sitting with jugs of beer in front of them, and looking very insignificant in their blue or brown Sunday best beside the women, whose holiday costumes made them look like brightly feathered hens. The old women ate cakes and drank possets as they sat and gossiped about the young people dancing. Had their friends wondered who'd do as a husband for whom, and who wouldn't do at all? Had they heard that so-and-so and so-and-so were soon to marry, though it looked as if it was all off between Bartosch's Franto and the smith's youngest daughter. . . ?

The musicians were up on a platform by the house wall; four empty casks, upended, supported it, and it was made of the two halves of a barn door that the village mayor had brought along for the purpose. The musicians played music for the dancing on their fiddles and flutes, not to mention the deep bass viol, and if they once left off to wet their throats, as they might well do, there were protests.

"Hey, you up there! Are you here to play for us or to drink?"

Krabat mixed with the young people of Schwarzkollm and danced boisterously with all the girls at random, now with this one and now with that. He danced with the singer too from time to time, as he did with all the rest, though it was hard for him to let her go away and dance with other young men. She understood that they must not give themselves away, and they talked mere nonsense, as one does while dancing. Only her eyes spoke to Krabat, though no one noticed that but him—and because he noticed it he avoided her glance when he could.

So it was that even the peasant women sitting by had no suspicion, and the old woman who was blind in one eye (it was only now that Krabat saw her) was no exception. However, Krabat decided not to dance with the girl any more after that.

In any case, evening soon came, the farmers and their wives went home, and the young men and girls went off to the barn, along with the musicians, to carry on the dancing on the threshing floor.

Krabat did not follow, thinking it wiser to go home now, back to the mill. She would understand.

He raised his cap in farewell, and felt something warm and soft on his head.

"Lobosch!" he suddenly remembered.

He knotted the corners of the napkin together, and then he stuffed it full of cakes and pastries from the abandoned tables.

11 · AN OFFER

AS WINTER approached it seemed to Krabat that time was passing more and more slowly; indeed, after the middle of November there were days when he had a feeling it was not passing at all. Sometimes, when there was no one near, he made sure he still had the ring of hair the singer had given him. As soon as he touched it in the pocket of his smock, he felt full of confidence. "All will be well!" he told himself, and somehow he was sure of it. "All will be well."

The Master had not often been away of late. Did he guess there was danger ahead; did he suspect something was going on behind his back, and he must be on his guard?

Krabat and Juro used the few available nights to go tirelessly on with their training of Krabat's will power, and more and more often Krabat managed to win their trials of strength.

As they were sitting opposite one another at the kitchen table one evening, Krabat happened to take the ring of hair out of his pocket. Idly, he put it on the little finger of his left hand. When Juro gave his next order Krabat did the opposite at once, and with astonishing speed and ease.

"Why, your strength seemed to be doubled all of a sudden!" said Juro. "How do you account for that?"

"I have no idea," said Krabat. "Perhaps it was chance?"

"Let's think!" Juro looked searchingly at him. "There must be *something* that helped you."

"But what?" Krabat wondered. "It can hardly have been the ring . . ."

"What ring?" asked Juro.

"This ring of hair. She gave it me on the Sunday of the fair. I put it on just now—but what could the ring have to do with it?"

"Don't say that!" Juro said. "We'll try it, and then we'll know."

They tried the ring and soon found that there could be no doubt about it. When Krabat put it on his finger, he could master Juro's will easily, and when he took it off, everything was the same as usual.

"That's quite clear!" said Juro. "With the help of that ring you're sure to beat the Master!"

"I can't understand it," said Krabat. "Do you think she can work magic herself?"

"Not the way *we* work magic," said Juro. "There's a kind of magic that must be learned with toil and difficulty, line by line, spell by spell, the magic of the Book of Necromancy; and then there's another kind that springs from the depths of the heart, from caring for someone and loving him. It's hard to understand, I know, but you had better trust that magic, Krabat."

The next morning, when Hanzo woke the miller's men and they went out to the pump, they saw that it had snowed overnight. The world around was all white, and once again the sight of the snow filled them with dread.

Now Krabat knew why; indeed, there was only one person in the mill who could not understand it, and that was Lobosch, who had not grown so very much larger since he came to the mill, yet was now a lad nearly seventeen years old instead of a boy of fourteen.

One morning, when Lobosch threw a snowball at Andrush in play, Andrush flew at him, and Krabat stepped in to stop a fight. Lobosch asked him what in heaven's name was the matter with them all.

"They are afraid," said Krabat, shrugging his shoulders.

"Afraid?" asked Lobosch. "Afraid of what?"

Krabat avoided a direct answer. "Be thankful that you don't yet know," he said. "You'll learn soon enough."

"What about you?" inquired Lobosch. "You're not afraid, are you, Krabat?"

"More than you guess," said Krabat. "And not for myself alone."

It was the week before Christmas when the Goodman drove up to the mill in the fen, and the men ran out to unload the sacks. The stranger did not stay on the box as usual; on this night of new moon he climbed down from the cart and went indoors with the Master. He walked with a limp. They saw the feather of his hat flicker behind the window pane, like a fire burning in the room.

Hanzo had torches fetched, and the men unloaded the sacks from the cart in silence and carried them to the grinding room. They tipped whatever was in them into the hopper above the Dead Stones, let the meal they had ground run into the empty sacks, and loaded them back on the cart.

At dawn the stranger came back to his cart alone and climbed up on the box. But before he drove away he turned to the miller's men.

"Which of you is Krabat?"

Coals of fire and bitter cold in one . . .

"I am!" said Krabat, stepping forward. Suddenly he could hardly swallow.

The driver of the cart looked him up and down, and nodded. "Good," said he. Then he cracked his whip, and away he went with his cart.

The miller shut himself up in the Black Room for three days and three nights. On the evening of the fourth day, the day before the Christmas season began, he summoned Krabat.

"I have something to say to you," he said, "and I don't suppose it will come as much of a surprise. You are still free to choose—for me or against me."

Krabat tried to act as though he knew nothing. "I don't understand," he said.

However, the Master did not believe him. "Don't forget that I know you rather better than you may like!" said he. "Many others have tried to set their will against mine over the years—Tonda, for example, and Michal, to name but two! Fools, idiots! But you, now, Krabat, I'd have thought you were wiser. If you want to be the miller here after me, you're the right man!"

"Why, are you leaving?" asked Krabat.

"I've been here long enough." The Master loosened his collar. "I want to be my own master! In two or three years' time you could take my place and teach the Black School. If you agree to that, I will give you all I leave behind, including the Book of Necromancy."

"And what will *you* do?" asked Krabat.

"I'll go to court!" said the Master. "I'll be a statesman, a Marshal, Chancellor to the King of Poland, maybe—it depends how the fancy takes me. All the great lords will fear me and the ladies will coax me to be their friend, because of my wealth and influence! All doors will be open to me, everyone will want me to advise him! As for those who dare defy me, I'll crush them underfoot—for I can work magic, and believe me, Krabat, I know how to make use of my power!"

He had worked himself up into a frenzy, his one eye was burning, and the blood had risen to his face. "You can do the same!" he went on, calmer now. "You can be Master of this mill for twelve or fifteen years, and then you can choose a successor from among your journeymen, give him all that belongs here, and you will be free to live a life of glory and renown!"

Krabat tried to keep a clear head, forcing himself to remember Tonda and Michal. He had sworn to avenge them—Tonda and Michal, and the others buried out on the Waste Ground, not forgetting Vorshula and Merten, Merten who might still be alive, with his wry neck, but what kind of a life was that?

He challenged the Master. "Tonda is dead, and Michal is dead too. Who's to say that I'm not to be the next?"

"I give you my word!" The miller held out his left hand. "My solemn word on it—and the word of the Goodman too. He has explicitly given me leave to promise you that."

Krabat did not take the offered hand.

"If it's not me," he asked, "will it be someone else?"

The Master moved his hand as though to wipe something off the table.

"It will always be someone," he said. "But from now on we could get together to decide who it is to be. Someone who wouldn't be missed, let's say—Lyshko, for example."

"I don't like Lyshko," said Krabat, "but he is one of my fellow journeymen, and am I to be guilty of his death? Or partly guilty, but I don't see much difference! No, miller, you will never get me to consent to that!" He had leaped to his feet, and now he shouted at the Master, loathing in his voice, "Make whoever you like your successor here! I'll have no part in it! I'm going!"

The Master kept calm. "You will go when I permit you! Sit down and listen until I'm done."

It was hard for Krabat to resist the temptation to try the strength of his own will against the Master's then and there; however, he obeyed.

"I understand your feelings," said the miller. "You're confused and surprised by my suggestion. So I'm giving you time to think it over at your leisure."

"Why?" asked Krabat. "I'll still say no."

"A pity." The Master looked at Krabat, shaking his head. "For if you refuse my offer, you *will* have to die. You know there is a coffin standing ready in the shed."

"Ah, but whose coffin?" said Krabat. "That we have yet to see!"

The Master did not move a muscle. "Do you know what it would mean if things turned out as you seem to hope they will?"

"Yes," said Krabat. "I could work no more magic."

"Well?" the Master asked. "Would you be content for that to happen?"

He seemed to be thinking for a moment, and then leaned back in his chair. "Well," said he, "I'll give you eight days' grace. In that time you'll have the chance to learn what life is like when you can work no more magic —I'll take care of that. All you've learned from me over the years—from this moment it will be gone, forgotten! And when the week is up, on the day before New Year's Eve, I'll ask you for the last time whether you want to take my place. Then we'll see if your answer is still the same!"

12 · BETWEEN THE YEARS

IT WAS a hard week for Krabat. He felt as if he were back in his early days at the mill. Every sack weighed as heavy as it really was, and it had to be carried from granary to grinding room and back to the meal-store. Krabat was spared nothing, now that he could not work magic, not a drop of sweat, not a sore place on his skin. Every evening he sank on his bed exhausted, but he could not sleep for hours. When you can work magic, you have only to close your eyes and recite a spell, and you are asleep at once, fast asleep for as long as you wish.

"It may be that I'm going to miss that worst of all," thought Krabat.

When he finally did fall asleep after lying awake so long, he was tormented by nightmares, and he knew they did not come by chance. He could easily work out who was sending him such dreams.

Dressed in rags, Krabat is struggling with a cart of stones, pulling it over the fields on the end of a rope. It is hard work in hot summer weather. He is thirsty, his throat dry as a bone, and there is not a spring of water in sight, nor a tree to give him shade.

The devil take that cart!

He is taking it to Blaschke, the cattle dealer of Kamenz, and he is working for a mere pittance. But a man must live on something, and ever since his accident—that was in Gerbisdorf, when he was caught in the machinery of the mill and it crushed his right arm to the elbow—ever since then Krabat must be glad of any work that comes his way.

So he drags himself along with the cart of stones, and he thinks he hears—or else he hears himself thinking it—he thinks he hears the Master's hoarse voice saying, "How do you like life now you're a cripple, Krabat? You might have been better off if you'd listened to me when I asked if you wanted to take my place at the mill in the fen! If you had the choice again today, would you still say no?"

Night after night Krabat dreamed that some such fate had overtaken him. He was old, or sick; he was in prison, though innocent of any crime; he had been pressed into the army, and he lay wounded to death in a wheat field, watching the crushed blades of wheat run red with the blood from his wounds. And at the end of these dreams he would always hear the Master's voice asking him, "Would you still say no, Krabat, if I gave you the same choice today?"

Only once did the Master himself actually appear in his dreams, and that was on the last night before his week's grace ran out.

To help Juro, Krabat has turned himself into a horse. The Master, dressed as a Polish nobleman, has bought him in Wittichenau market for a hundred guilders, along with his saddle and the halter. The horse is handed over to him.

The Master rides him pitilessly over the moor, over sticks and stones, over hedges and ditches, through thorns and mire.

"Remember that I am your master!"

The miller brings the whip down on him, driving the spurs into his flanks. Blood is flowing from them; he feels it run warm down the inside of his thighs.

"I'll teach you!"

A gallop to the left, a gallop to the right, then on to the next village. A tug at the reins, and they stop outside a smithy.

"Hey there, smith—where the devil are you hiding?"

The smith comes running up to ask what the gentleman wants, wiping his hands on his leather apron. The Master swings himself out of the saddle.

"Shoe me this horse, and shoe him with red-hot iron!" says he.

The smith cannot believe his ears. "With—with red-hot iron, sir?"

"Must I tell you everything twice? I'll teach you to work faster!"

"Barto!" The smith calls for his apprentice. "Take the reins and hold this gentleman's horse!"

The smith's apprentice is a freckled urchin who might be Lobosch's brother.

"And take the heaviest shoes you have!" the miller tells him. "Show me your stock!"

The smith leads him into the forge, while the boy holds

the horse, talking to him in Wendish. "Quiet then, old horse, quiet, now—why, you're all of a tremble!"

Krabat rubs his head against the boy's shoulder. "If I were free of the halter," he thinks, "I could try to save myself..."

The boy sees that the horse is hurt; the leather strap has rubbed a sore place by his left ear.

"Just a minute," says he. "I'd best loosen the buckle a bit. It won't take a moment."

He loosens the buckle, and pulls the halter off over the horse's head. As soon as he is rid of it, Krabat turns into a raven. Croaking, he rises in the air and makes for Schwarzkollm.

The sun is shining in the village of Schwarzkollm, and below him he sees the singer standing near the well, a straw basket in her hand, feeding the chickens, when a shadow passes over him and he hears the cry of a hawk in his ear. "The Master!" Krabat thinks at once.

Swift as an arrow, wings spread, Krabat swoops down, down into the well, where he changes into a fish. Will he be safe now? Too late, he realizes that he is trapped; there is no way out of the well.

"Singer!" he thinks, directing all the power of his mind at her. "Help me out of this well!"

The girl dips her hand into the well, Krabat becomes a narrow gold ring on her finger, and so he comes back into the world above.

Suddenly there is a nobleman dressed in Polish clothes standing by the well. He has only one eye, and he wears a red riding coat with silver lacing and black galloons.

"Can you tell me where you got that pretty ring, young woman? Let me see it..."

He is stretching out his hand, reaching for the ring . . .

Krabat turns into a grain of barley, slips from the girl's finger and falls into the basket. As she scatters the next handful she throws him among the chickens.

And suddenly the man in the red coat is gone. There is a strange rooster, black as coal, with only one eye, pecking at the corn—but Krabat is faster. Seizing his advantage, he turns into a fox. Quick as a flash he falls on the black rooster and bites through his neck.

There is a crackle of chaff and straw between his teeth . . . nothing but chaff and straw.

When Krabat woke he was bathed in sweat. He found that he had bitten into his straw mattress and was gasping for breath. It was some time before his heart stopped thudding.

He took his defeat of the Master in his dream as a good omen, and now he felt sure he would win, and the Master's days were numbered. He, Krabat, would put an end to the miller's evil deeds—he was the man appointed to break the Master's power!

That evening he went to the Master's room. "My answer is still the same!" he said. "Make whoever you like your successor! As for me, I refuse your offer."

The Master heard him out quietly. "Go to the woodshed," said he, "and get yourself a spade and pick. There's a grave to be dug out in the fen—that will be your last task."

Without replying, Krabat turned and left the room. When he reached the shed, a figure emerged from the shadows.

•

"I've been waiting for you, Krabat. Am I to take word to her?"

Krabat took the ring of hair from the pocket of his smock. "Tell her you carry a message from me," he said. "Tell her that tomorrow, on the last evening of the year, she may go to the miller and ask for my freedom, as we arranged." And he described her house to Juro. "If you show her the ring," he went on, "she will know that you come from me. But don't forget to tell her she is free to come to the mill or not to come. If she comes, that is good—and if she doesn't come it is good too, since I won't mind what happens to me then."

He gave Juro the ring, embracing him.

"Promise to do as I say? You won't persuade her to do anything she doesn't really want to do?"

"I promise," said Juro.

And a raven with a ring of hair in its beak set off on its flight to Schwarzkollm. Krabat went into the shed. Was that the coffin standing in the corner? He shouldered his pick and spade and trudged through the snow, out into the fen, until he came to the Waste Ground.

He found a place where a dark rectangle stood out in the white snow. Was it meant for him, or did it mark the Master's grave?

"About this time tomorrow," thought Krabat, driving his spade into the ground, "about this time tomorrow we will know."

The next day, after breakfast, Juro took his friend aside and gave back the ring, telling him he had talked to the girl, and it was all settled.

That evening, at dusk, the girl from Schwarzkollm came to the mill, wearing her communion dress, with the white band around her forehead. Hanzo opened the door to her and asked what she wanted, and she asked to speak to the miller.

"I am the miller!"

Thrusting his men aside, the Master came out to meet her. He had on his black coat and three-cornered hat, and he was pale, pale as death. "What do you want?" he asked.

The girl looked steadily at him. "I want my young man!" said she.

"Your young man?" The miller laughed, an evil, bleating sound, like a billy goat laughing. "I don't know your young man!"

"His name is Krabat," said the girl, "and I love him."

"Krabat?" Now the Master was trying to bully her. "Why, young woman, do you even know the man? Could you pick him out from among my other journeymen?"

"Yes, I know him," said the singer.

"Anyone can say that!" The Master turned to his men. "Go into the Black Room and stand in a row, side by side, and don't move!"

Krabat expected that they would have to turn into ravens now. He was placed between Andrush and Stashko.

"Stay where you are, and don't any of you make a move! Not you either, Krabat!" said the Master. "At the first sound I hear you make, she dies!"

He took a black cloth from his coat pocket and bound it around the girl's eyes. Then he led her in.

"If you can show me which is your young man, you may take him away with you!"

Krabat was horrified; he had not expected this. How was he to help her? Even the ring of hair was no use now!

The girl walked up and down the row of the miller's men, once, twice. Krabat could hardly stand upright. He felt that his life was lost—and hers too! He was overwhelmed by such fear as he had never felt before. "She will die, and it's my doing!" he kept thinking. "My doing . . ."

Then the singer, who had walked up and down the row of journeymen three times, put out her hand and pointed to Krabat.

"This is the man," she said.

"Are you sure?"

"Yes," she said, "I am sure." And with that it was all over. She untied the cloth from her eyes and went up to Krabat. "You are free," she said.

The Master staggered back and leaned against the wall, while the men stood where they were, as if turned to stone.

"Fetch your things from the attic, all of you, and be off with you to Schwarzkollm!" said Juro. "You can spend the night in the loft of the village hall."

The miller's men came back to life, and crept out of the Black Room. The Master, they all knew, would not live to see New Year's Day. At midnight he must die, and the mill would go up in flames.

Merten, with his wry neck, pressed Krabat's hand warmly. "You've avenged Tonda and Michal, and all the others too!"

Krabat was dumb, unable to say a word. But the girl put her arm around his shoulders, and wrapped him in her shawl of wool. It was warm, soft and warm, like a cloak of safety around him.

"Let us go, Krabat."

He let her lead him out of the mill and through the fen, away to Schwarzkollm.

At last, when they saw the lights of the village flicker out between the tree trunks, one by one, he asked her, "How did you pick me out from the others?"

"I could feel that you were afraid," she said. "You were afraid for me, and that was how I knew you."

As they walked toward the houses of the village, snow began to fall, very gently, fine flakes of snow like flour falling on them from some great sieve.